The Setting Sun

'7.50

Barrett

THE

SETTING SUN;

OR,

DEVIL AMONGST THE PLACEMEN.

Published, August 20th 1809.

THE

ETTING SUN;

OR,

L AMONGST THE PLACEMEN.

TO WHICH IS ADDED,

NEW MUSICAL DRAMA;

BEING A PARODY ON

THE BEGGAR'S OPERA,

ELY ACTED, WITH UNIVERSAL ECLAT, AT THE

EATRE ROYAL, GLYSTER PLACE;

WITH

S FOR A MASQUERADE JUBILEE,

ON A GRAND SCALE.

CERVANTES HOGG, Esq.

IN THREE VOLUMES.

ike thieves, surpris'd whilst they divide the prize,
seeming doubtful where their safety lies."

D'AVENANT.

VOL. I.

London:

Printed by J. D. Dewick, 46, Barbican,

HUGHES, 35, LUDGATE-STREET; CHAPPEL, PALL
; GRAY AND SON, PICCADILLY; KIRBY AND CO.
OXFORD-STREET; BLACKLOCK, ROYAL
EXCHANGE; AND WILSON,
ROYAL EXCHANGE.

1809.

POSTSCRIPT.

ALTHOUGH when this work was written some weeks, and part of it months since, yet the author had very little doubt of something like the consequences which have been announced this day (September 23) to the public in the newspapers.

One article contains a notice of a *hostile* meeting having taken place between Lord Castlereagh, attended by Lord Yarmouth, and Mr. Canning, attended by a Mr. Ellis. On the second fire, Mr. Canning was severely wounded in the thigh.

This is indeed

The Devil among the Placemen!

The other article we shall extract *verbatim* and *literatim* from the Times newspaper, without making any comment whatever on it :—

" Yesterday the Middlesex Jury found a bill of indictment, for a conspiracy, against Mary Anne Clarke, Francis Wright, and Daniel Wright, for an attempt to defraud Col. Wardle of the price of certain household furniture sent to Mrs. Clarke's house in Westbourne Place. The bill was found upon the evidence of Major Dodd, Mr. Glennie, and other respectable witnesses; and warrants were directed to issue for the apprehension of the accused parties, in order to take their trial at the next Middlesex Session. Col. Wardle was under examination nearly three hours."

CERVANTES HOGG.

TO

G. L. WARDLE, Esq. M. P.

As HONEST TRAY was guarding the door of his master, a yelping pack of hungry curs endeavoured to drive, or seduce him away, by threats, or cajolings; but *Honest Tray* lifted up his leg, showered down a plenteous stream of contempt upon the insidious curs, and remained firm to his duty.

CERVANTES HOGG.

ADDRESS

TO THE

BRITISH PUBLIC.

" So Justice, whilst she winks at crimes,
Stumbles on innocence sometimes."

HUDIBRAS.

HIS Majesty's Ministers having kindly con-
descended to recommend to us, for our rule
of conduct, that " *it is inconsistent with the
principles of British justice to pronounce
judgment without previous investigation ;*" we
beg leave to second their recommendation, in
the case of Colonel Wardle, to whom it is as
applicable, and more justly due than to the

VOL. I. b

the *Cintra Convention-Mongers*. Gratitude
should rather incline us to think well of the man,
who has braved a host of corrupt peculators
for your sakes, than to believe a woman, who,
from her own confession, subsists on the pro-
fits of adulterous prostitution, and wreaks her
vengeance on all those who have the courage
to resist her extravagant demands. It would
be well for you to reflect before you suffer
yourselves to be led away to damp the ardour
of such a man, and consequently of all men
of similar patriotic principles, and commit a
suicide on your country.

It would be an insult to common under-
standings to lose time in pointing out to you
the state-tricks, and barefaced attempts, which
have been put in practice to prejudice the
public mind against their benefactor. When
we witness the Attorney General assailing,
from the Treasury Benches, the veracity of

Mrs. Mary Anne Clarke, when adduced against the Duke of York, and immediately afterwards, in Westminster Hall, gravely admitting and enforcing the evidence of the very same *incredible* witness against Colonel Wardle, the most charitable opinion that can be entertained of such contradiction is, that an Attorney General must have, at once, an *official* and a *professional conscience*, which are perfectly reconcileable, although as opposite as black and white. As the lawyer says to Hudibras :—

> " But you may swear, at any rate,
> Things not in nature, for the state;
> For in all courts of justice here,
> A witness is not said to swear,
> But to *make* oath, that is, in plain terms,
> To *forge* whatever he affirms."

Let us see what oaths were *made* against Colonel Wardle. Mrs. Mary Anne Clarke *makes* oath, that " she was to give the

Colonel every information in her power, to assist him in the investigation of the conduct of his Royal Highness the Duke of York; in return for which, he was to furnish her house as part of the requital she was to have for her services."—But, before the House of Commons, she unequivocally declares *(upon her honor!)* that "she is actuated neither by malice, nor the hopes of gain;—that she neither has received, nor expects to receive, any remuneration for her testimony." How can we reconcile these two extremes, Mrs. Mary Anne Clarke, but in the words of Hudibras's epistle to Sidrophel?

> "—— that you have try'd that nothing's borne,
> With greater ease than public scorn;
> That all affronts do still give place
> To your impenetrable face,
> That makes your way through all affairs,
> As pigs through hedges creep with theirs;

Yet, as 'tis counterfeit, and brass,
You must not think 'twill always pass;
For all impostors, when they're known,
Are past their labour, and undone.''

Colonel Wardle, a gentleman of *acknow-ledged* HONOR, also denied that " he ever induced her to give her testimony by any promise of reward."——Now, it happens luckily for Mrs. Mary Anne Clarke, that, not having been examined *on oath* before the House of Commons, this self-contradiction is, in the eye of the law, only *prevarication*; had it been otherwise, a jury would, in all probability, have deemed it *perjury*.——Yet (strange to say!) this witness, who was not worthy of credit in the House of Commons, when her veracity was unimpeached, was allowed to be a competent witness in Westminster Hall, when she was contradicting herself in the grossest manner, and in the very *gist* of the action, the promise of reward by furnishing her house!

> " I would not give, quoth Hudibras,
> A straw to understand a case,
> Without the admirable skill
> To wind and manage it at will;
> To vere, and tack, and steer a cause,
> Against the weather-gage of laws,
> And ring the changes upon cases,
> As plain as noses upon faces,
> ·As you have well instructed me,
> For which you've earn'd (here 'tis) your fee."

Well—who comes next to *make* oath? Mr. Daniel Wright, *brother to the plaintiff*, Mr. Francis Wright!—When Mrs. Mary Anne Clarke was *turned up* (as the *keeping* phrase is) by her *royal friend*, she was indebted to Mr. Francis Wright between five and six hundred pounds; and, on her application to him to credit her for the furniture necessary for her house in Westbourne Place, he refuses, until she tells him she has a friend

in view, who, *she believes*, will be responsible
for the payment. This friend was Colonel
Wardle. It was impossible for him to have
carried his point, without subjecting himself
to the pecuniary demands of Mrs. Mary Anne
Clarke, under the genteel term of *loans ;* and
to have refused attending the haughty dame
on her shopping excursions, would have, in
like manner, disappointed all his views. He,
of course, nods assent to an invitation from her
to accompany her to see some furniture which
she is about to purchase, and to approve her
taste in the choice of the articles. This (as Col.
Wardle alleges) is the sole ground of the
responsibility charged upon him.—When
they arrive in Rathbone Place, Mr. Francis
Wright *happens* to be in his bed, *luckily for
him*, (as he himself observes in his appeal to
the public) or he *should have lost the evidence
of his brother, Mr. Daniel Wright.*—Now,

without this evidence, so luckily in the way, there would have been nobody to have proved Mrs. Mary Anne Clarke's nods, winks, and hints, the Colonel's giving his opinion on some of the articles she had selected, and the *inference* of his being the friend, who was to pay for them.—Who does not know that a tradesman, furnishing goods to *ladies* of a *certain description,* ought to have, and indeed is very seldom without his *eye-teeth* about him ? but we doubt whether Colonel Wardle's example will not prove a loss to such trades-men in general, as gentlemen will, in future, be very cautious of accompanying *ladies a-shopping,* and paying compliments to their taste !

> " Ideots only will be cozen'd twice ;
> Once warn'd is well bewar'd.''
>   DRYDEN.

The friend who, according to Mrs. Mary

Anne Clarke's *hint,* was to be responsible for
the furnishing of her house in Westbourne
Place, was expected, and, no doubt every
preparation was made to receive him as——a
gentleman—a colonel in his majesty's service,
and a M. P. A prettier *train of evidence*
could never have been laid to blow up a man.
There were a plaintiff, two *disinterested* witnesses, (one of them the *immaculate* Mrs.
Mary Anne Clarke, who had baffled the fire
of the whole ministerial phalanx, including
the crown-law-officers) and a defendant with
money in his pockets. Mrs. Mary Anne
Clarke had so *enfiladed* the *colonel* that, if he
did not *capitulate upon terms,* she could
oblige him to *surrender at discretion.*

Now for the *denouement!*—After the investigation, Col. Wardle, in strict conformity
with his declaration, that the motives of his
visits to Mrs. Mary Anne Clarke were solely

for the purpose of bringing public abuses to light, drops all correspondence with her. Enraged at his ungallant behaviour, and, what was more galling, disappointed in her rapacious views, she gets Mr. Francis Wright to make, G. L. Wardle, Esq. M. P. debtor for goods ordered by him for Mrs. Mary Anne Clarke, in Westbourne Place. When the bill is presented, the colonel is astonished, and denies, in the most positive manner, any idea of making himself respon- sible. He, accordingly, resists the demand, *despises the sort of evidence*, which is to be brought against him, and, in an over-con- fidence of victory, sustains a defeat.

> " Democritus ne'er laugh'd so loud,
> To see bawds carted thro' the crowd,
> Or funerals with stately pomp
> March slowly on in sullen dump,
> As *Moll* laugh'd out, until her back,
> As well as sides, was like to crack."
>
> HUDIBRAS.

It has been thought that, as Col. Wardle was undoubtedly indebted to Mrs. Clarke for his popularity, it would have been no great sacrifice, if he had settled this affair; but who, that has heard Mrs. Clarke's own account of herself, can for a moment suppose that the sacrifice would have ended there? No; Mrs. Clarke is a skilful angler, who only plays with a fish to drag it more securely to shore. How could Col. Wardle have acquiesced in a demand, grounded on a prior promise of remuneration, consistently with his declaration in the House of Commons? The fact is, that the cleansing of the Augæan Stable was but *boy's play* to his undertaking, and it was almost impossible that he should wade through such a miry slough, without having a single speck of dirt on his clothes.

But what stain hath all the ingenuity of

the ministerial phalanx, and crown-law-officers been able to bring forward to his prejudice? Why truly, that he has been tricked
by that mistress of tricksters, *Mistress* Clarke,
into a responsibility for a debt, incurred, if
it ever was incurred, for the public benefit!
On that very account, the public ought to
support and countenance him more than
ever; or never deserve to find another bold
and intrepid assertor of their constitutional
rights. Do, *Mister Bull*, only place your-
self in Col. Wardle's arduous situation, and
if you do not, upon reflection, vote him your
everlasting gratitude, we pray thee to let us
hear no more talk about *British liberality
and generosity*.

To sum up all:—Notwithstanding the
most injurious reports of the Duke of York's
conduct had been long afloat, and had occasioned great discontent in the nation in

general, among the army in particular, no man in the House of Commons would *honestly* dare to prefer charges against the second son of his sovereign, except Col. Wardle. Nay, every one of them, out of tenderness to the royal family, *affected* to believe that the charges could never be substantiated. One member was instantly visited with a *vision* of a *foul conspiracy to overturn the constitution,* and pretended to see (with a sort of scotch *second sight*) *treason and sedition at work*— (he might easily have seen corruption and peculation): Another held over the colonel's head, like the sword of Damocles, the threat of *infamy,* if the charges were not substantiated; and the whole nation were set grinning by another (of *notorious principles*) who tenderly warned the colonel against lending himself to an *unprincipled association.* As some kind of a proof of it, he called *himself* the *colonel's friend.* Col. Wardle, however, was not to be intimidated ; he was even com‑plimented by some of the ministerial party on the fairness and firmness with which he had discharged his duty to the public, and the gratitude of the whole nation poured in upon him. " Now," says *Mistress Clarke,* " is my time. Colonel Wardle owes all his popularity to me ; and, if he closes his purse-strings against me, I will nip it in the bud." Has she been able to do so ?—No; she has only exhibited herself in all her naked, hideous deformity; a cloak of simplicity óver a lump of putrescence. What bounds could Col. Wardle hope to set to her extor‑tions, when not satisfied with the thousands such a reptile has been suffered to expend of the public money, she extorts thousands more for the suppression of the Duke of York's letters ; and, as if her appetite became more voracious with the quantity of *golden food* lavished upon it, she now threatens to publish the letters (*real or manufactured*) of all her other admirers, and to gratify her rapacity at the expence of the domestic happiness of a number of families. Such harpies the poet well describes:—

> "They snatch our meat, defiling all they find,
> And, parting, leave a loathsome stench behind."
>
> DRYDEN.

Let *Mistress Clarke* gull a few *sensual* individuals in future, if any will fall into her trap after being so well forewarned of the Circean Cup; but Johnny Bull must be a driveller indeed, if he suffers himself to be gulled by her affected simplicity, after having been admitted to peep behind the curtain of her boudoir, and even behind her bed-curtains, at the army lists and applications for

preferment pinned to them, unless he would
wish to incur that censure of the poet:

> " 'The world is nat'rally averse
> To all the truth it sees or hears;
> But swallows nonsense and a lie,
> With greediness and gluttony."
>
> HUDIBRAS.

The truth, once out, can never be recalled,
and none but fools will shut their eyes and
ears against conviction. If, after the present
lesson, we should still witness an archbishop,
and shoals of deans, prebends, doctors in
divinity, *wise* legislators, generals, colonels,
&c. dancing attendance at a prostitute's *levée*,
for a share in the public spoils, or to *bribe
her to silence*, we may venture to predict
that—ENGLAND'S SUN IS SETTING.

CERVANTES HOGG.

THE

SETTING SUN.

———

" Sometimes some fam'd historian's pen
Recalls past ages back agen ;
Where all, I see, through ev'ry page,
Is but how men, with senseless rage,
Each other rob, destroy, and burn,
To serve a priest's, a statesman's turn ;
Tho' loaded with a diff'rent aim,
Yet always *asses* much the same."

SOAME JENYNS.

" I HOPE," said Oliver Cromwell, on read-
ing a letter of Admiral Blake, of his hum-
bling the Spaniards at Malaga—" *I hope
to make the name of an Englishman as
great as ever was that of a Roman!*"—
Degraded as we now are from our brave
ancestors, at least with respect to public virtues, there are yet to be found many, many

Englishmen, who are animated with the purest sentiments of patriotism, and who would willingly devote their property and lives to the interest and honor of their country. But what encouragement is there for such men to step forward, when barely to hint at what all the world sees and sneers at us for—that things are all going the wrong way, is enough to draw a reprimand on the first body of men in the universe?

Lord Chesterfield, at the beginning of the present reign, writes thus :—" The sons of Britain, like those of Noah, must cover their parents' shame as well as they can, for to retrieve its honor is now too late. One would really think, that our ministers and generals were all as drunk as the patriarch was. However, in your situation, you must not be Cham, but spread your cloak over our disgrace, as far as it will go."—If this had not been a letter from one courtier to another, who—

" *Nothing woo, but gold and power*"—

we should have said that his lordship was right in his premises, but wrong in his conclusion. His lordship has *ingenuously* laid open his own putrid heart, and that of a politician in general. Their sole aim is to keep the cancerous sores of the constitution from being probed, and to spread their cloaks over them, to prevent the *corrupting maggots*, that is to say *themselves*, from being discovered to the naked eye of the public. We, who are no courtiers, think that, to spread a cloak over corruption, is to patronize and encourage it; that to open the *louse-bag*, is to destroy the insidious vermin that are momentarily undermining the constitution; and that it is the duty of every well wisher to his country to uncloak knavery. He should exclaim boldly, such and such men—

" *Objiciunt noctem fraudibus.*"

Veil their frauds with darkness.—

If a self-interested, hungry administration, either play themselves, or, through weakness,

B 2

suffer others to play the *morbus pediculosus*
with the constitution, and eat their way into
the public vitals, they should be exposed,
and no king, who has a grain of sense, will
suffer them any longer to lead, or rather mislead him. Sir William Temple once ob-
served in person to King Charles II. who
was suspected of wishing to introduce the
same religion and government as that of
France, that he never knew but one man, and
that one a Frenchman, named Gourville, who
understood the English nation well; that
when he (Sir William) was at Brussels, in the
first Dutch war, and Gourville heard that the
parliàment grew weary of it, he said that the
king had nothing to do but to make peace;
that he had been long enough in England,
and seen enough of its court, people, and
parliaments, to conclude—" Qu'un roi d'Ang-
leterre, qui veut être l'homme de son peu-
ple, est le plus grand roi du monde; mais
s'il veut être quelque chôse d'avantage, par
Dieu, il n'est plus rien."—In plain English :
" That a king of England, who wishes to be

the man of his people, is the greatest monarch on earth ; but if he wishes to be somewhat more, by G— he is no longer any thing."— Is it worth while, then, for a king of England to be *the man of his people*, since his merely being so will make him the *greatest monarch on earth?* Certainly, if there are any charms in monarchy.—*Reges pro nobis, non nos pro regibus*—Kings were made for us, not we for kings—is an axiom that stupidity itself must allow.—Hence, then, comes that art of ruling which, though galling to the pride of kings, is nevertheless gospel—that there is no absolute power but that of the laws—and that the king who establishes despotism, is himself but the *slave* of *slaves.*—By way of illustrating this point, let us see what is the character of a despot. Knox, in his history of Ceylon, thus describes its arbitrary prince, or rather pest—" He sheds a great deal of blood, and gives no reason for it; nor is he content to take away men's lives, but he puts them to long and lingering torments; for when he is displeased with any, he will command to cut and pull away their flesh with pincers, and burn them with hot irons, to confess their accomplices; which, to rid themselves of the torments, they will readily do, and accuse many they never knew nor saw. Then he will order their hands to be tied about their necks, that they may eat their own flesh, and so lead them through the city to execution; the dogs, who are used to it, following them to devour their flesh. At the place of execution, which is always the largest highway, that all may see and stand in awe, there are always some sticking upon poles, others hanging up in quarters upon trees, besides what lie upon the ground, killed by elephants or otherwise. He hath a great many prisoners, whom he keeps in chains; some in gaol, others in the custody of great men, and for what, or how long, no man dare inquire. Some are allowed food, others not; and if they do any work to relieve their want, if he knows it he will not permit them; because, as he says, he puts them there to torment and punish them, and

not to work and be well maintained ;—yet this
is connived at, and there are shops by the
prisons to sell their wares. When the streets
by the palace are to be swept, the prisoners,
in their chains, are let out to do it. When
they have been long in prison, at his pleasure, without any examination, they are led
to execution; nor is his anger appeased by
the death of the malefactor, but he oftentimes
punishes all his generation : sometimes killing
them all together, and sometimes giving
them all away for slaves ; and thus he usually
deals with those whose children are his at-
tendants; for, after they have been at court
a while, and know his customs, he cuts off
their heads, and puts them in their bellies,
no man knowing for what crime. When
they are killed, they are styled rebels and
traitors, and their fathers' houses, lands, and
estates seized on for the king's use, which are
sometimes redeemed by giving fees to the
courtiers, but often the whole family and
generation perish."—Such is the picture of
an imbecile, a brutal and unenlightened

tyrant! Now which is the more appropriate appellation for this fiend—A prince of men, or a dog of dogs? Does this monster possess a shadow of the Divine attributes of the Supreme Power—justice and mercy? No— no—Are his subjects made after God's own image? No; they are disfigured by slavery, whose base insignia make them rather resemble Milton's fallen angels. Those naturalists are undoubtedly right who maintain that there is a gradation from man to beast, and throughout nature, of which every link of the chain is evident. The freeman is of an order as much superior to the slave, as the slave is to the ourang-outang.—Now for the picture of a conqueror! The ourang-outang of Ceylon, cruel as he is, has not dyed his hands in human blood a thousandth part as deep as the ourang-outang, which, issuing from the wilds of Corsica, has ravaged, and still continues to deluge the whole Continent of Europe with blood. Who could believe that the once generous, magnanimous, polished, and scientific French nation, after

having felt the invigorating and divine glow
of freedom, would stoop their necks to a
foreigner, an obscure adventurer, and the
blood-thirstiest despot that ever scourged the
world? To a monster who slaughtered thousands of disarmed and unresisting prisoners
of war; who poisoned thousands of his own
wounded soldiers, and buried thousands more
with the dead, smothering them with quick-
lime to drown their groans, and get rid of
them without trouble; who fled, like an ar-
rant poltroon, from Egypt to France, leaving
his brave, deluded followers in the extremity
of danger and distress; who afterwards mur-
dered Admiral Villeneuve and Marshal Brune,
for not commanding, what Sir Sydney Smith
had taught him that he himself could not
command—success in war;—who would have
wreaked his cowardly vengeance on Sir Sydney
Smith, then a prisoner of war, if he had not
eluded it by stratagem; and who actually did
assassinate the brave Captain Wright, also a
prisoner of war, whom it was his duty to have
protected?—Who, we repeat, could have

believed that the once generous, magnanimous, polished, and scientific French nation could not only stoop their necks to such a blood-thirsty despot, but could place their glory in aiding him to devastate Europe, and lay its liberties under his cloven foot? The present wanton aggression of Spain, will be an eternal blot upon the French character. Spain has been, for years past, every thing that France could wish her to have been—her ally—her friend—her purse-bearer—her milch-cow——her, I may almost say, slave; for if the magnanimous Spanish nation did not bow their necks, its rulers did, and that was tan-tamount. What pretence, then, is there for devastating the face of her country, and making her rivers and streams flow with blood? Why, truly, to put Joey, a lawyer's clerk, on the throne of Spain? And is then the glory of France so connected with a lawyer's clerk, that her best blood—that blood which had once nobly flowed for her own independence—is to be spilt to enslave a friendly nation?—

" Who conquers, wins, by brutal strength, the prize—
" But 'tis a glorious work to civilize :"—

Tickell.

Yes, France, inglorious France, having lost
all her trade, manufactures, and commerce,
and submitted to the yoke of a foreign up-
start, would rejoice, in order to cover its own
ignominy, to see the universe brought under
the same disgraceful subjection, and to have
the *honor* of *being the first of slaves.*—Can
Frenchmen be so blind to their own real condition, when—

" ———— E'en beasts disdain
" The den's confinement, and the slavish chain,
" And roar to get their liberty again —?"

Creech's Luc.

They may boast in the bulletins of deeds
which, at a future period, they will wish
could be for ever blotted from the annals of
European history; but all their impostures
cannot conceal from the world the ignomi-
nious marks on their necks of their oppres-

sor's galling chain.—Their situation is so exactly like that of a dog——but stay—we will have the story in verse, if our Pegasus be not as *foundered* as a certain ex-chancellor of the treasury, and lord high chancellor, who, it is said, are so greased in the heels for want of exercise, as to have lost their stomachs for hopping, ever since they hopped out of office.

THE CUR AND MASTIFF:

AN ALLEGORICAL FABLE.

A GALLIC CUR so savage grew,
At ev'ry pair of heels he flew;
　Ne'er was there such a curst dog!
His master e'en was not secure—
So muzzled him, to make things sure,
　And made him wear a huge clog.

But as the *Gallic* custom is
Disgrace to hide with lofty phys,
　Loth to betray their mischance;
So cur, no less a fool than devil,
To other dogs scorns to be civil,
　And bids them keep their distance.

The canine race each other jog,
To see the muzzle, chain, and clog,
　With laughter nearly choking:
But still the vicious cur they fear,
Though trammel'd worse than dancing bear,
　And dread to pay for joking.

Encourag'd by their slavish fears,
The cur resum'd his wonted airs,
　　And cried: " *Vive mon bon maitre!*
" Of all men he be *le plus grand,*
" And I'm his dog—so *allemand!*
　　" Who bows not is *un traitre.*

" *Le maitre grand—le chien grand,*
" We make de world dance saraband,
　　" As ye drive sheep before ye :
" No man and dog dis world did see,
" Arrive at such a pitch as we,
　　" Of human, canine glory.

" Behold! *dis* chain, and *dis medaille,*
" Distinguish me from de *canaille,*
　　" And speak de wearer's *bonheur :*
" For laurels, which my brows bedeck,
" These emblems mark, about my neck,
　　" *La Legion de Honneur.*

" *Mon maitre and moi, nous reglons the roast,—*"
" Bl—t you! sneak off, and cease your boast—"
Roars out an ENGLISH MASTIFF:
" We see how painfully you jog,
" Beneath that muzzle, chain, and clog,
　　" Fit punishment for caitiff."

" Under a cruel butcher's yoke,
" By stealth defenceless lambs you choke,
  " And live on stolen mutton :
" But when a brave and equal foe
" Presents—you like not fighting—no—
  " At that sport you're no glutton.

" My sons a bold and hardy race,
" As they the past events shall trace,
  " Will shout a free dog's glory :
" But thine will swell with honest rage,
" And try to blot out from the page,
  " The black, disgraceful story."

Reader, the moral, in plain prose, is this :
—No chief can attempt the conquest of other
nations, without first enslaving the country
which he governs : therefore, the *glory* of a
conqueror is a disgrace to his own, as well as
to every conquered state. To contribute to
such a man's success, is to glory in slavery ;
and, for a momentary intoxication, damn
one's self to everlasting infamy !
The French have defeated and trampled
upon all the surrounding nations of Europe,
except that of sea-girt Britain. Whence has

arisen this vast success? The cause is evident. We read, in Jones's Life of Bishop Horne, that certain insects (the African ants) set forwards sometimes in such multitudes, that the whole earth seems to be in motion. A corps of them attacked and covered *an elephant* quietly feeding in a pasture. In eight hours, nothing was to be seen on the spot but the skeleton of that enormous animal, neatly and completely picked. The business was done, and the enemy had marched on after fresh prey. *Such powers have the smallest creatures acting in concert!* This case is exactly in point: the ant had one instinctive impulse—a struggle for food to preserve existence; the French nation rose *en masse* to assert their natural liberty, without which life itself is no value: the immense bulk of the elephant could avail nothing against the spirit, fire, and incessant attacks of its individually contemptible, collectively irresistible, enemy; the heavy continental nations, torpified into slavery by ecclesiastical and regal tyranny, fell prostrate at the feet of the enthusiastic French legions. But where the French were opposed by men of similar mould, fighting for the same cause, for that cause for which they had for ages contended, their efforts were vain, and oftener recoiled on their own heads than otherwise. The French armies have now totally lost sight of that *glorious cause* in which the present war originated; they are now fighting from the *basest* of *motives*—like slaves, sacrificing their lives to gratify the ambition of a foreign tyrant, and, like robbers and assassins, cutting throats for rapine and plunder. Their numbers are, however, so thinned by these incessant exertions, and the population of France so drained, that the scale seems to hang, if not preponderate against her, if she do not soon abandon her *maniacal policy*. Woe then be to her!

Conquest, natural levity, and vanity, may blind Frenchmen to their true glory and interest, and reconcile them to that state to which a Briton would prefer death: " Disguise thyself as thou wilt," says Sterne, "still,

SLAVERY! still thou art a bitter draught!"
Frenchmen have been slaves during so many
ages, that they did not know what true
liberty was when it was in their power; they
preferred licentiousness, of which, with their
natural fickleness, they soon grew sick, and
fell again into its opposite extreme—*abject
slavery.* They would now degrade all mankind to their own level; but there are nations
(the British in particular, whose birth-right
is freedom, whose inheritance is liberty) who
cannot suffer palpable impositions on their
judgment, persons, and property, without
resistance, nor wear the galling chains of
slavery without seeking to do themselves justice. They will perish before they will submit, and against such resolution, and such
resources as they possess, France will waste
her strength in vain. For what end then ?
For the glory or interest of France? Let us
see how it can be for either :—1st. *Can a continuance of warfare be for the glory of
France ?*—No, not with all the blunders,
ignorance, and stupidity of British ministers,

generals, and convention-mongers on her side.
France threw down the gauntlet by a silly
gasconade that Britain dared not to engage
with her *single-handed*. Britain has engaged
France, with almost all Europe and America
to back her, for several years, and with ad-
vantage : There's French glory for you !—
France boasts to all her satellites, that Britain, the sovereign of the sea, is under
blockade, and that she will not make peace
without having ships, colonies, and freedom
of commerce restored to her : Britain actually
blockades the whole coasts of France and her
allies ; so that scarcely a ship dares skulk out
into the open ocean, and manifests to the
world, that France shall neither have ships,
colonies, nor commerce, unless she make
peace with the world, or, in plain English,
without her permission: There's French
glory for you! At the late meeting at Erfurth,
the Emperors of France and Russia *styled*
themselves the two greatest monarchs in the
world; like the two swordsmen in *Bessus,*
who gave it under one another's hands that

they were the two bravest men in the world!
This *oil of fool* might go down glibly at
Erfurth, but would only make an Englishman smile, and relate the following very appropriate anecdote :—When the Earl of Stair
was ambassador in Holland, he made frequent
entertainments, to which the foreign ministers
were invited, not excepting even that of
France, though hostilities were then commencing between the two countries. In return,
the French resident as constantly invited the
English and Austrian ambassadors upon the
like occasions. The French minister was a
man of considerable wit and vivacity. One
day, he proposed a health in these terms:
" *The Rising Sun*," (alluding to the motto
of his master, Louis XIV.) which was
pledged by the whole company. It then
came to the Baron de Riesbach's turn to give
a health, and he, in the same humour, gave
"*The Moon and Fixed Stars,*" in compliment
to the Empress Queen. When it came to
the English ambassador's turn, all the eyes of
the company were fixed upon him; but he,

no way daunted, drank to his master by the name of "*Joshua, the Son of Nun, who made both the Sun and Moon stand still.*"— What would French glory say to this? France may bestow the appellation of *The Army of England* on a division of its forces, which has dared to advance so far as the heights of Boulogne, but has prudently stopped there. She may term a parcel of crazy boats "*The Invading Flotilla;*" although, wherever they have ventured rashly to the harbour's mouth, they have been driven under their land batteries by a single gun-brig. Yet, whenever she has wanted employment, she has preferred to pick a quarrel with, and fall upon Portugal, Spain, Sweden, or any other little power, and pilfering from them, to a struggle with Britain for the empire of the world: And there rests the chapter on French glory for the present!—We now come to the second point: *Can a continuance of warfare be for the interest of France?* No; though they might continue for a few years longer, merely to draw their

c 3

public expenditure from exhausted Europe, as sturdy paupers glean among the stubbles. French vanity would make France the mistress and emporium of the world; but Britain stands in the way—the only rival, and a successful one. In arms, Britain yields to none, having maintained her sovereignty of the sea, and more than once baffled the power of France, backed by almost all the forces of Europe, America, and of several Asiatic princes. In arts and sciences, particularly in the fine arts, Britain at least divides the palm, but in agriculture, manufactures, and commerce, she leaves all competition far behind : There's the sting.—— Britain's wealth is the envy of France; but not being able to cope with her in the legitimate pursuits of it, she affects to despise them as a nation of shopkeepers, and exclaims—" *Delenda est Carthago*."—It is well known that, after the destruction of Carthage, there were no longer any bounds to the ambition of the Romans, who trampled upon the necks of mankind. If Britain

were to be humbled, France would play the
same game over again, and the world would,
too late, deplore its having been, not passive
spectators, but active contributors towards its
downfall. Let us suppose, for a moment,
that France should prevail to the fullest
extent, she could never hope to raise so
proud a superstructure as that which she
would have overthrown, unless she could
persuade herself that she could inherit the
public spirit, perseverance, enterprise, industry, and good faith of Britons, just as
the Tartars absurdly believe, when they kill
an enemy, that they possess themselves of all
his great qualities. Emulation is a noble,
generous passion, which strives to equal or
excel by fair competition alone: envy is a
blind, grovelling passion, which would foully
destroy what it has not merit enough to enter
into competition with : to the former, Britain
owes her prosperity; to the latter, she may
set down the rancorous hatred of France, or
rather of her Corsican ruler. Has not the
despot avowed to the world that trade and

commerce should be annihilated, rather than the British should engross so large a share of it!—Has he not, in pursuance of this *fiend-like project*, interdicted the commerce of Europe, and of the United States of North America? Is this for the interest of France, of Europe, or the United States? Let their wants, deprivations, distresses, and wishes for returning peace, speak to the question.—When did ever a *conqueror* benefit society? When did a *conqueror* appear but as a scourge not only to the state cursed with his sway, but to all the adjacent ones? The instruments of Divine wrath, they are protected until they have effected their mission, and are then abandoned to the horrors which they themselves have occasioned in others. Almost all Homer's heroes perished through treacherous friends, relatives, or adulterous wives. Cyrus united the kingdoms of the Medes and Persians; subdued the Assyrians; took Babylon; overthrew the Lydians, making their king Crœsus prisoner; restored the Jews, who were captives in Babylon, to liberty, and was the first emperor of the Persian monarchy, which continued till the time of Alexander the Great, two hundred and seven years afterwards. Yet, leading his troops against the Scythians and Massagetæ, he was slain with two hundred thousand followers, in an ambush, by Queen Tomyris, who, to revenge the death of her son, caused his head to be cut off and thrown into a vessel full of blood, with this bitter taunt: " *Satia te sanguine, quem sitisti.*"—Satiate thyself with blood, which thou hast thirsted after. ALEXANDER the Great (Butcher, we should add) overthrew DARIUS and the Persian empire, and because he did not ravish his mother, wife, daughters, or concubines, he is extolled as a pattern of continence and greatness of soul. And yet this little wry-necked fiend had his Bagoas, and his Thais, to please whose whim he laid Persepolis, the noblest city in the east, in ashes. He was also a drunkard, who, when inflamed, was capable of murdering his best friends with his own hands; and, even in cold blood, could assassinate, or expose to the most cruel torments, his ablest generals, even those to whom he chiefly owed his victories;—who, ·without any plausible pretence to cloak his ambition, ran about the world like a mad-man, spreading death and desolation around him; deluging the earth with human blood; exterminating nations, or reducing them to the most abject slavery and misery. Rats-bane, at length, did the world justice upon him.——CÆSAR enslaved his country by her own arms, and rivetted her chains by the most infamous prostitution of his own person: he was the husband of every wife, and the wife of every husband in Rome; but the dagger of his dearest friend, Brutus, avenged her wrongs.——LOUIS XIV. (also nicknamed *le Grand*) affected universal dominion, and kept Europe embroiled for years to attain to it: yet he lived long enough to see fortune frown on all his hopes—to sink into the slave of the mountebank Scarron's widow, and to die devoured by lice, leaving France more circumscribed than he found it.——

CHARLES XII. of Sweden, was evidently
born to be a scourge to mankind, and he
carried on his game (in the language of conquerors—*his career of glory*) until Sweden
had lost all her foreign provinces, and had
neither trade, money, nor credit. Her vete-
ran troops had been either killed, or had
perished through want, or were in a worse
situation, above one hundred thousand being
slaves in Muscovy, and as many more among
the Turks and Tartars; and the very species
of men was so visibly decayed in the country, that there were not sufficient for culti-
vating their lands!!!

> " When kings, by their huffing,
>   Have blown up a squabble,
> All the charge and cuffing
>   Light upon the rabble."

Are nations such fools as not only to submit tamely to the sanguinary pranks of these
monstrous madmen, but even to put fire-
brands into their hands, and assist them with
their lives and fortunes? Yes—they are—

" ———————— these slaves,
The wide-mouthed brutes, that bellow thus for freedom ;
Oh ! how they run before the hand of pow'r,
Flying for shelter into ev'ry brake ;
Like cow'rdly, fearful sheep, breaking their herd,
When the wolf's out, and ranging for his prey !"   OTWAY.

And all this cowardice too, at a time when
they might instantly stop the maniac by
saying—" We have defended our own ter-
ritories, and justice demands that we should
not attack those of our neighbours."—If he
will go on, let him go *alone* and be d———d
—he will not go far.

This is no speculative theory : We have
all witnessed the inefficacy of kings going to
war, when not joined by the hearts of the
people, in the Italian States, Dutch Provinces, Germany, and Russia ; and we are
much mistaken if we shall not yet find, to
our cost, that same inutility in other states.
The old system is moth-eaten, and kings have
had a severe lesson, that the sullen apathy of

an insulted people, is more dangerous than an open insurrection. If men are to be asses of burthen, the devil may drive; one tyrant is as good as another. To be a king in fact, is to govern men indeed—*freemen!*

If the reader should require any more examples that conquerors have been the same pests in all ages, let him turn to almost any page of history, of any nation, and he will find that there have always been from one to half a dozen insignificant individuals blustering and hectoring it over *five* or *six hundred millions* of souls—*souls!* no, *bodies without souls!* Were history only to record the actions of princes who have benefited mankind, it might be comprized in somewhat less space than the walnut-shell, which is said to have contained a complete copy of Homer's Iliad; and we cannot see why any others should be handed down to posterity, unless, indeed, by way of gibbeting them, as we serve murderers, *in terrorem*;—but there are thousands of volumes to prove, that mankind, in all ages, have been *fools.* What can their *foolish wars* prove else ? The Grecian princes carried their whole forces beyond sea—for what purpose ? *to recover a libidinous, run-away adultress !*—

> "———————— a lustful wife,
> The dear-bought curse, and lawful plague of life ;
> A bosom serpent, a domestic evil,
> A night invasion, and a mid-day devil."

Well ; they destroyed the city of Troy, and all its *innocent* inhabitants, to punish the *guilty* Paris ; (very just this indeed !) and having spent ten years in this notable exploit, they returned home *cuckolds*, as might have been naturally expected, and most of them were slain by the paramours of their wives : Bravo !—They went out to revenge one cuckold, and all came back

> "———— *in their old confines, with forked heads.*"
> SHAKESPEAR.

as will ever be the case with those fools who do not *look at home.*

Alexander and Cæsar fought for *ambition*, which is the destruction of millions for the vanity of one person—

> " How vain a creature were the plotting knave,
> But for easy fools !"
>
> TATE.

Even the *heathen* Virgil exclaims—O cursed wars ! *(bella horrida)* and we shall pass them over as such, to make way for what the *Christians* (soi-disant, but mal-faisant followers of the mild doctrines of Christ) term *holy wars*, (a devilish good joke !) but which were as bloody as the most *infernal wars* that ever the world witnessed.

> " —————— True religion
> Is always mild, propitious, and humble ;
> Plays not the tyrant, plants no faith in blood,
> Nor bears destruction on her chariot wheels ;
> But stoops to polish, succour, and redress,
> And builds her grandeur on *the public good.*"
>
> MILLER.

In real fact, these wars sprung only from the accursed policy of the Roman pontiffs, who wished to make a parade of the vassal princes whom she could send abroad from their states, on *spiritual concerns*, at her nod, whilst they condescendingly took all the trouble of managing their *temporal affairs* at home, and plundering their subjects—

> " ———— Fools as gross
> As ign'rance, or bigotry made drunk."

The oceans of blood shed in the subsequent *religious wars* and *massacres* had much the same origin—the knavery of few, and the folly of many. When fanaticism has phrenzied the brain, sectaries, like red hot iron, are to be wrought up to the temper of any cool-headed fellow, whether prince, priest, or coal-heaver; and, if they are not confined, by some superior temporal power, to their liberal method of cursing and d——g each other to the lowest pit of hell, they will fight for the love of God, like two blackguards for a belly full. A fanatic, therefore, let loose upon the world, is a destroyer of the

human race ; but tie up his hands, and none
so great a propagator—

> " ——— each female saint he does advise,
> With groans, and hums and ha's, and goggling eyes
> To rub him down, and make the spirit rise :
> While, with his zeal transported, from the ground
> He mounts, and sanctifies the sister's round."
>
> LEE.

The priests, therefore, claim the supremacy
of all other warriors ; because what the world
loses by them in one respect, they make up
in another. There are to be met with in
history, an infinity of other causes for spilling
human blood ; but they are deemed less *honorable* than the foregoing ones : such as
when two kings contend for a bit of barren
land, which belongs to neither, and is worth
nothing to neither of them ; when a queen, a
royal mistress, is jealous of the power of a
minister, who is no war minister, and wishes
to force him out ; when a minister hates the
queen, or royal mistress, and, being a war
minister, wishes to keep himself in place in

spite of them ;—when a king wants money, and declares war to squander on his private debaucheries the supplies raised for the nation's defence; when a hypochondriac king anticipates the devil's claim, and requires some amusement.—Yes, reader, you may stare; but the serious game of warfare has really been played, like a game of chess, for the royal amusement.—In our English history, several of our monarchs have even had *pawns* on the board. Edward III. *pawned his jewels* to pay foreign forces;. the Black Prince *pawned his plate;* Henry V. *pawned his tables* and *stools of silver*, which he had from Spain; Queen Elizabeth *lost* her jewels; nay, Henry V. *pawned* his imperial crown once! and Edward III. three times!!! To such petty *three blue ball* shifts have these mighty conquerors been driven, after having drained their miserable subjects to the dregs to make themselves glorious! And what becomes of all their *glory* at last? Why, it is generally laid at the feet of demireps. Omphale made Hercules spin; Achilles preferred Briseïs to the cause of Greece; Thaïs inflamed Alexander to fire Persepolis; Cæsar was the drudge of every woman in Rome; Louis XIV. married the mountebank Scarron's widow; and a certain *English hero* has been a *milch-cow* to C—y, C—le, C—ke, C—ll, C— and Co.——Such *glory* is, indeed,

> " —————— the vain breath
> Of fools, and sycophants."
>
> LANSDOWNE.

Reader, do not imagine that we would jest. with heroes;—no, no, 'ware *edge tools!* We would only remark, that it is " *pitiful—wondrous pitiful*," such brave men should not knock their " *knotty pates*" together for some more rational *cause*—such as the *just* and *necessary* contest in which we are at present engaged, and which, with the help of *God*, we will discuss, till we shall be able to cry—" hold—hold!" with honor—

> " —————— the soldier's treasure, bought with blood,
> And kept at life's expence."

But when we hear of black Pongo's spar-
ring with black Cohadjee, and copper-
coloured Malatchi's setting to with copper-
coloured Attakulla, for a trifling quantity of
rum, tobacco, shot, powder, rifles, &c. is
not the practice of these whom we stigmatize
as savages, rather below the dignity of the
crowned heads of civilized, polished Europe,
the seat of the arts, sciences, and all terres-
trial wisdom ?—But what signifies what thou,
reader, and I think of it;—kings are made
of other stuff: we may as well whistle jigs to
a milestone, as expect them to hop to our
measures. In short, *ambition* is an incurable
madness : What is it but

> " ——————— desire of greatness?
> And what is greatness but extent of power—
> But lust of power, a dropsy of the mind,
> Whose thirst increases while we drink to quench it,
> Till, swoll'n, and stretch'd by the repeated draught,
> We burst and perish."

Ambitious tyrants are therefore mere *bubbles*, which, after having, for a short time,

rode triumphant on the stream, " *burst and perish.*" As Europe has such a scourge at present upon her hands, the best advice seems to be that which Durandante gave to Monte-sinos, as Don Quixote relates his adventures in the cave: " *Patience, and shuffle the cards.*"

> " Remember—he's a man; his flesh as soft,
> And penetrable as a girl's ——
> A surfeit, nay, a fit of common sickness,
> Brings this immortal to the gate of death."
> LEE'S ALEXANDER.

The *bubble* must burst, and it is only to see it out. Few conquerors have left any immediate descendants; still fewer have left their conquests to their descendants; and, by God's blessing, for the repose of mankind, not one of them has ever transmitted his troublesome spirit to his descendants; so that it is only a *lease for life*, which, in few instances, has been suffered to run out to its natural length.—Patience, therefore, and reflect that

D 3.

" ———— *Levius fit patientiâ*
Quicquid corrigere est nefas."   HORACE.

The nature of *revolutions* have been elegantly paralleled to a boiling pot, with which the scum flies uppermost. We do not understand how this *aristocratic* epithet can be applied to any part of the human race, without an insult to the Creator; and as this *scum* generally developes men of strong mind, too long depressed by *prejudices*, it were time to lay aside these prejudices, and consider personal merit in its proper rank—that is, above all the fortuitous circumstances of birth, rank, or affluence. If rightly considered, revolutions are the thunderstorms which clear the political horizon, when darkened by tyranny, pride, superstition, or ignorance. They are not always to be deprecated, as this country has experienced one, to which the term *glorious* has been, and justly too, annexed. May we not read in them the hand of God, which overthrew the tower of Babel, to shew the inefficiency of man to perpetuate his labours?

4

May we not see in them the hand-writing on the wall, the " MENE, MENE, TEKEL, UPHARSIN," the end of the government of *light-weight* princes? Who, that has read the Scriptures, can peruse the annals of Europe for a century or two back, and wonder that there are so many king *Nebuchadnezzars* of the present day turned to grass? Or that an attorney's clerk should wear a crown, when David was a shepherd boy?—*Bravo!* We may all have a chance in time, and we pledge our veracity against the reader's modesty, that there is not a man in the creation, who will say, at least who will think, with *Sancho Pança*, that his scull is so misshapen, that " should crowns be suffered to rain down from heaven, not one of them would fit it;" but rather,

" *Regem me esse oportuit.*"

I should make a very pretty sort of a king.

Indeed, we are so accustomed to the sight of *simple* kings, that almost any *simpleton* might venture to put his head into a crown without blushing much deeper than if it were his worsted nightcap. Voltaire tells us, in his history of Charles XII. of Sweden:—" Few are the princes whose actions merit a particular history. In vain have most of them been the objects of slander or flattery: small is their number whose memory is preserved, and would be yet smaller, were the good only remembered."—We would propose an easy method for future historians to preserve a continuity of reigns, and yet not to bestow more upon insignificant princes than just such a mark as farmers stamp upon the backs or sides of their sheep: for instance—they might have *Charles*, the *Cuckold*—*Paul*, the *Madman*—*Catherine*, the *Concupiscent*—*Alexander*, the *Lackwit*—*Gustavus*, the *Giant-Killer*—*Ferdinand*, the *Credulous*—*Francis*, the *Forsaken*—*Frederic*, the *Foolish* and *Fallen*—*Napoleon*, *Nick's Friend*, &c. ——By this mode, as vanity is a ruling passion, kings would behave decently for their own sakes, in order to have a somewhat more

honorable niche in the temple of historic
fame. Historians and poets have more to
answer for than they are aware of. Of this
opinion, too, is Butler, himself a poet, and
inferior to none.

> " Surely our authors are to blame,
> For making some well-sounding name
> A pattern fit for modern knights,
> To copy out in frays and fights :
> Like those that a whole street do raze
> To build a palace in its place ;
> They never care how many others
> They kill, without regard of mothers,
> Or wives, or children, so they can
> Make up some fierce, dead-doing man,
> Composed of many ingredient valours,
> Just like the manhood of nine tailors !"
>
>   HUD.

Varnishing over vice with well-turned pe-
riods, or glozing over royal crimes with
falsehoods, as a cat covers up what it leaves
with ashes or dust, is not their only, nor
worst, though a very usual and heinous
offence. They can do no service to the dead

criminal; but they injure posterity by making princes unborn believe, that curst ambition is thirst for glory, prodigality regal splendor, haughtiness true majesty, their people slaves, and the public purse their own. Kings may take our honest words for it, that all such writers are lying knaves, who only jest with them, to share in preying upon their subjects:

> " Gross flatt'ry can alone by *fools* be borne,
> For it implies at once disdain and scorn:
> Well managed praise may still expect success,
> Praise shews esteem, whene'er it shews address:
> ...... *fools* gross flattery can brook,
> ...... the bait, and can't suspect the hook." DENNIS,

...... pect any thing from those
...... of sycophants and poets,
...... the opinion of the
...... an interest in
...... word may be
...... Although
...... upon kings and
...... ever was a cus-

tomer at our shop for a penny. Perhaps the reason is, because we do not deal in flummery. The poet laureat is the *court fancy-dress maker:* we are contented with cutting out for the *swinish multitude;* who, as despised as they are, *pay all the reckoning.* It is, therefore, reasonable that they should see how their money goes, and protest, remonstrate, petition, or address, against any mismanagement of it; and kings should, *wise ones would,* listen to them, not with others ears, but with their own, and pay attention to them too!—So will they prosper accordingly. Thus say *we ourselves.*

Now, without pretending to any Divine revelation, or even a vision, except that which passes over the *" mind's eye"* upon a retrospect of the past, we will venture a little bit of a (not prophecy) guess into what may be, and we will add to it our pledge to the public, that our skill at prescience is, at least, upon a par with that of the present M——y. We have seen, in France, the end of a dynasty of *absolute monarchs;* and of a degenerated race of nobles, from the indignation of a long enslaved populace; we have beheld nearly the whole of the German circle of princes, as well as those of Italy, sent to grass, through the apathy of their subjects, occasioned by the weakness of their governments; we have beheld the emperor of Russia, with a retinue of courtiers, who grew sick when they found an essential difference between a court and a camp, and with a herd of boors, to whom liberty was unknown even by name; we have beheld him, we repeat, commencing his career as the defender and avenger of insulted Europe, and ending it by becoming an abject vassal, nay, an instrument of the ambition and vengeance of the tyrant.   Lastly, we have endeavoured to instil somewhat of our own enthusiastic love of independence, into the Spaniards and Portuguese: but, alas! they have been so long enslaved by a branch of the same dynasty of *absolute monarchs* as the French, and by

hordes of ignorant bigots, that, having little
or nothing of their own to contend for, they
care not who is their next master :

"——————— another, and another still succeeds,
And the last *fool's* as welcome as the former!"

We have witnessed all these things—we say
—Well, what then? demands the reader.
Why, we add, that we have witnessed
enough to convince us—nay, even kings
themselves, who oftener lose their heads than
their prejudices, that the *public esteem* is the
sole prop of every government, when put to
the trial; and, as a man's esteem is not to be
gained, like a spaniel's, by kicks and thumps,
he should be treated with decency at least, if
not with attention and civility. We add,
too, that the study of the history of past
events is only an idle amusement at best, if
not a waste of time, unless applied to the
amelioration of our own conduct, by obser-
vation and amendment upon the faults of
others. Buonaparté was wise enough to be

2

aware of the force and prevalence of *public opinion*, and he began with Spain by making its reigning monarch, and his successor, and indeed the whole of (to him detested) race of Bourbon, despicable to the nation. We will venture an opinion, that if Carlos or Ferdinand had remained firm in their capital, and thrown themselves into the arms of the nation, by making their cause the people's, and the people's theirs, they would have made a glorious, and, with the aid of the British, a successful defence. But when the king, queen, and princes, had so indelibly disgraced themselves and the nation, as to leave the kingdom, and to throw themselves at the feet of a known despiser of all honor, to accuse, nay abuse, and request his protection against each other, what great veneration could be expected either for themselves or their mandates, issued by their *creatures*, whose highest prospect of reward for victory, held out to the nation to be inspirited, was that of *having things restored to their former situation!!!* Why, the nation cannot be in a worse situation than its former one; and this was a notable incentive to prodigies of valour! What is *true valour?* We subscribe to the poet's idea of it:

" It is the greatest virtue; and the *safety*
Of *all mankind*; the object of its *danger :*
A certain mean 'twixt fear and confidence;
No inconsid'rate rashness, or vain appetite
Of false encount'ring formidable things,
But a true science of distinguishing
What's *good* or *evil.* It springs out of *reason,*
And tends to perfect honesty; the *scope*
Is always *honor,* and the *public good:*
It is no valour for a *private cause.*"

The proclamations of the *Junta* against the *liberty of the press* sufficiently explained that the people were not to be cured of their blindness; and they have remained in it till the mist (that is, their host of oppressors) has been chased away. The conqueror has seen the errors of the *Junta,* and has shewn that he knows well how to profit by them; he knows that his own strength lies in the weakness of his opponents, and their weakness in a contempt of the people. He, therefore, assumes those virtues to which he is a total stranger as well as themselves. He *feigns* to respect the *public good* and *public opinion;* and whatever any *westward* ho! *writers* may say, it is morally certain that the condition of the Spaniards must be ameliorated, even if Buonaparté should subdue them, since we find that he deems it necessary to his own views to hold out to the people, that their situation will be better under his, than the Bourbon dominion. Read his IMPERIAL DECREES: he abolishes the inquisition and feudal rights, and reduces the number of convents to one-third!!! If these are not what (in a strict sense of the rules of descent of the Spanish crown) may be termed Imperial Decrees, being undoubtedly the *ipse dixit* of an usurper of the Spanish crown, they are, nevertheless, DECREES *worthy of an Emperor!* And, although by these means Buonaparté may think to bolster up his own ill-gotten power, yet to give the Spaniards a glimpse of civil and religious liberty, is the

surest method to make them assert their rights
to both, even against himself!! According
to the old saying—" Give him rope enough,
and he will hang himself."—But this, in all
human probability, may be a work of time,
and therefore " *patience and shuffle the
cards.*"

We will venture another trifling guess,
which, however, is much more probable
than the prophecies of *Mr. Brothers*, because built on the *rational premises* we have
before mentioned; which is—that Buonaparté will not only profit by his pretended
respect for the *public good and opinion*, but
that he has it in contemplation to take advan-
tage of another weapon, weak in itself, but
overwhelming in the hands of a multitude;
namely, *superstition* and *credulity!*—Alexander, (the great hero, but little man) not contented to subdue the *bodies* of men by his
arms, sought to tyrannize over their minds
by palming his *divine origin* upon them:
The Roman emperors pursued the same *state-*

trick: the popes made a pretty penny of the *gates of heaven*: Mahomed did wonders through his *seven heavens*, his *flying ass*, and his *houris*: Cromwell held the sword in one hand, and the Bible in the other: Buonaparté, in Egypt, was a Mussulman, predestinarian, sent by the prophet to deliver his brother Turks from the tyranny of the beys; he is, now, also a Roman Catholic, and has possessed himself of St. Peter's keys; (think of that and tremble, all ye rebels against his power—to be buffetted by him in this world, and to have the gates of heaven shut against you in the next!) and he now tells the Spaniards, in case they reject his *brother Joey*, that " he shall place the crown of Spain upon his own head, and cause it to be respected by the *guilty*;—for GOD *has given him power and inclination to surmount all obstacles ! ! !*"

Here's a *divine mission* for you—and a *thundering prophet*, with a vengeance!— before whom the degraded Continent—

" ———— bow their heads with homage down,
And kiss the feet of this exalted man :
The name, the shout, the blast from ev'ry mouth
Is *Buonaparté!—Buonaparté* bursts
Your cheeks, and with a crack so loud,
It drowns the voice of Heav'n : Like dogs you fawn,
The earth's commanders fawn, and flatter him :
Mankind starts up to hear his *blasphemy ;*
And if this hunter of the barb'rous world
But wind himself a *god,* you echo him
With universal cry."

LEE's ALEXANDER.

Impudence and luck are a sufficient stock
at any time for a prophet, and the little great
man has enough of both. The sapient pro-
fessors of a certain German university have
already shoved him up into *Orion's Belt ;*—
and as he never knows when to stop, there
will be fools enough ready to take his own
word that his place is yet higher. But however much to the taste of Turks, Copts, and
Arabs, may be the massacres, robberies, and
lies, with which the coming of the Corsican
prophet amongst us, have been marked, being
conformable to, though rather more out-

E 2

rageous than, the progress of their own Mahomed; yet we should imagine they can never be accredited by the followers of the doctrines of the meek, humble, and beneficent Jesus Christ. We hope so, and pray that our *Catholic brethren* of *Ireland* will not (to use a very homely though appropriate figure) *cut off their noses to be revenged upon their faces;* but will have *patience and shuffle the cards*, till our enemies shall have less power, and our ministers more sense, when we may all reasonably expect more tolerance, and fewer taxes:

> Good Heav'n! we pray thee quickly send the time,
> Authors may feed on somewhat else than rhyme;
> And all mankind serve thee in their own way,
> With plenteous boards, and moderate to pay!
> Then each light heart may chaunt—*God save the King;*
> But now we *fast* and *pay* too much to sing.

Buonaparté will, in the end, serve as another eternal proof, that the Almighty Father of the universe will not permit any earthly tyrant, however dignified, to wrest from him

the absolute dominion, which belongs to himself alone, over his creatures.

Waiting for such a happy change in the
tide of our affairs, but with a very faint
prospect of it for the present, we will proceed
with our *guess* :—If Buonaparté succeed in
Spain, (of which the most sceptical can now
scarcely entertain a doubt) he will attempt to
humble to his feet, or associate to his views
against Great Britain, all the rest of Europe,
by a partition of Turkey, through which
country his way will be clear to Persia and
the Indies. Nay, in all probability, the
National Institute of France may be, at this
moment, employed in making a digest from
the Persian and Sanscrit languages, and in
tracing the pedigree of the *Corsican Buona-
partés* to *Shah Abbas*, or *Vishnu*, according to
the *Mussulman* and *Hindoo* laws.—Having
once established a kind of *family compact*
with his Mussulman and Hindoo brethren,
he hopes, by their means, to inflict, at least,
a desperate wound on the British empire in
India, if he shall not be able to glut his

revenge by its total annihilation. We trust
that Buonaparté's expedition to Egypt; his
embassy to Persia.; his *unguarded* threats of
stabbing Britain in India, as well as on the
Continents of Europe and America; will sufficiently bear us out with. every *reasoner*
against the charge of being a *visionary.* We
have all *dreamed* too long; it is now time to
open our eyes to the light of the sun. If
Buonaparté should succeed in his embassy
to Persia!—It is reported that he has suc-
ceeded—Well, whence comes this art of
his, of alienating, the confidence of all
nations, Christian, Mussulman, or Hindoos-
tanee, from his adversaries?—Why—he has
skilful agents with each—no boobies, without
any other pretensions than high birth and
fortune, but men of *talents*—(no—hang that
word—it has been too much burlesqued!)
men of judgment.—Our *civil list* is so *scanty*,
that when an ambassador is wanted, the question is *not* who has the greatest diplomatic
genius, but who has the longest purse, and
the ambition to shine at a foreign court *at*

his own expence. This may be economy; but it is of that foolish sort proverbially denominated *penny wise* and *pound foolish.* Buonaparté knows this well.

His *secret service-money* is expended on men capable, and who dare not neglect to fulfil his orders, which are to blacken us in every court in Europe, and throughout America; it is never squandered on *rotten borough-mongers, contractors, agents,* with their useless hordes of relatives, bastards, parasites, dependants, mistresses, valets, &c. &c. He does, indeed, expend some money on *opera-girls*; but then he sends them to amuse the emperor of Russia, or *condescendingly* permits them to emigrate to England, whither they are generally accompanied by their *chers amis,* who are often his *agents!!!* There are, at this moment, some of them in this country, who confessedly receive salaries from him, not indeed as *espions,* but, *à couvert,* as notes of admiration of their musical abilities. These people, although commonly the dregs of their own country, are received into the

E 4

first families in this with open arms; extract
all secrets, of public as well as private concerns, in return for a song; and—*make Buonaparté laugh!!*

THEY MANAGE THIS BETTER IN FRANCE!

It is only by *looking at home* that we can
afford to be *generous abroad.* Not all the
wealth or power of Great Britain can regene-
rate the Continent; a change in the principles of their governments can only effect
that *desideratum.* Here's how.

THE KING, SHEPHERD, AND CUR.

KINGS from the people spring, not they from kings,
The heads these are, and those the underlings ;
But for the good of those, these called to sway,
Those for their good alone submit t'obey.
Hence kings are guardians of the public weal,
Bound to pursue it with their utmost zeal.
Who deem their pleasures are their sole concern,
This fable suits—so, let them read, and learn.

BEHRAM, a Persian king who thought his throne
Not for his subjects rais'd, but self alone,
In indolence repos'd with regal glare,
And left his people to his vizier's care.
The end was natural—where masters sleep,
The stewards fatten, and the tenants weep.
Relying on the monarch's love of ease,
The vizier only sought himself to please ;
Relations, friends, and parasites he fed,
Ne'er once regarding how the people bled.
Corruption was the order of the day,
The troops grew negligent thro' want of pay ;
Sedition's hollow murmur grew more loud,
And dire impends rebellion's thick'ning cloud.
Too late the clamor reach'd the royal ear,
T'avert the storm was now his only care.
Pensive he stroll'd the fields, at ease to think
On means to stop him on destruction's brink.

As thus employ'd, a shepherd struck his view
Hanging a dog; the monarch swiftly flew
To ask the cause of treatment so severe :—.
" His crime is black," replied the clown austere;
" Behold a traitor, and a traitor's due!
" I rais'd and fed him; but the cur untrue
" Betray'd his trust—nay with the wolf combin'd,
" To thin the flock to his defence consign'd.
" Caught in the fact, the wily villain dies—
" No less a sentence justice will suffice."

The king his own imprudence now discern'd—
This truth important from a shepherd learn'd :
That kings should look into their own affairs,
Nor trust to others' eyes, and others' ears.
Of cur and vizier similar the deed,
A sim'lar punishment the king decreed.
Such an example of their pow'rful chief
Struck terror into ev'ry lesser thief;
Economy brought order in her hand,
And scatter'd happiness throughout the land.

Such should have been long ago the fate of
the Prince of Peace, and hundreds of others,
generals as well as ministers of the continental
power. We have been grossly deceived in
the Spaniards, and have mistaken the procla-

mations of some few powerful individuals, struggling to keep their hoards and offices, for the voice of the nation. Alas! they have been long immersed in deeper shades of igno-. rance than Egyptian darkness itself. Buonaparté knows them to a hair. In his 22d bulletin he says, that " the British, in their flight, killed all the horses that were over fatigued or wounded, and which might em-. barrass their retreat. It is scarcely credible (he adds) how that spectacle, so shocking to our manners, of hundreds of horses shot with pistols, is *revolting to the Spaniards*. Many persons look upon it as a sort of *sacri-fice*—some *religious rite*, which gives rise, in the minds of the Spaniards, to very strange pictures of the *religion of England!!!*"— We may laugh at this most execrable non-. sense, if we please, but Buonaparté, we shall find, will frame a handle of this con-. temptible tool to carve out for us the invete-. rate hatred and detestation of the ignorant and bigotted Spaniards, who really know no, difference between protestantism and pa-

ganism.——In the 23d bulletin, Buonaparté
himself points out our errors to us : " France
(he tells us) was stirred up and supported by
the unanimous resolution to re-assert rights
of which she had been deprived in times
of obscurity :—In Spain, a few men stirred
up the people, in order to preserve the exclu-
sive possession of rights odious to the people.
Those, who fought for the Inquisition, for
the Franciscans, and for feudal rights, might
be animated by an ardent zeal for their *personal interests*, but could never *infuse* into a
whole nation, a *firm resolve* or *permanent
opinion*."—Our *political Quixotes*, however,
would have a brush with the *windmills*, and
have been laid sprawling in the dirt : Five
millions of money, and five thousand of
the best troops in the world sacrificed !—
Oh !—

" 'Tis the time's plague, when MADMEN lead the BLIND !"
                              SHAKESPEAR'S KING LEAR.

Buonaparté has now leisure enough to
preach up to the Spaniards that we have
        2

abandoned them, after inflaming their passions, to all the horrors of an unsuccessful resistance. He tells us that our retreat had exasperated them against us, and that their difference of language, manners, and religion, contributed not a little to that disposition of their minds; yet we are going to offer up *another sacrifice* to such gross superstition!—He tells the Spaniards that they must refund all the money which we have sent to them, and yet we are about to remit more! He will permit them to receive our gold and silver; but will take care to make them shut their ports against our soldiers. In the latter instance, he will show a greater respect for our brave troops than we shall evince for them ourselves, in hazarding them once more against superstition and ignorance, in addition to superior forces, and all the other disadvantageous circumstances of warfare.

Baffled and *bubbled* in every one of our continental subsidies, we should now husband all our resources to enable us to outlive a struggle, of which Heaven alone can see the

end. It is a *war* of *finances*, which, on our
part, can only be met by *political economy*
and *private industry*. In the latter we abound;
in the former we are so notoriously deficient,
that it may be as well to consider how far we
are from the brink of the gulph. We have
only to look to ourselves. The Continent
cannot long remain in its present lethargy,
from the natural order of things in this revo-
lutionary world. Tyranny begets liberty;
liberty ease; ease refinement; refinement
luxury; luxury effeminacy; and effeminacy
slavery, and consequently tyranny again.
For which reason, and from feeling the pulse
of the present times, we prescribe the following recipe, in plain English, instead of the
Warwick-lane Latin, which, by the bye,
Celsus himself could not read, if resusci-
tated, and become president, elect, senior
fellow, or candidate of the said college :

TAKE of *political economy and honesty*
(not *Burke's* Jesuitical sort) of each two
drams; of *patriotism* (take care of the

bastard species, denominated *Broad-bottomed*, which is rank poison) three dràms; of *energy* and *foresight* (beware of that entitled *Old Woman's*, growing in *Portland-Isle*) of each two drams; of *common sense* (not the *legalis* or *conventionalis* sort) two drams.

☞ The above medicines may not effect an immediate cure, but will be an infallible remedy if made into pills, with a quant. suff. of *conserve* of *patience*, (to be found all over the British Isles) and taken in doses suited to the constitution, fasting.

John Bull.—Fasting! I hate the very sound. Fasted only t'other day; pretty near come to't every day, I think; fasting never was suited to a *British Constitution*.

—— Why no, *good Johnny*; but then you know political, as well as p—— doctors always recommend it, that their patient's pockets may have a guinea when they come to dip their hands into them.

John Bull.—Aye, why shou'd n't have

too many drains at once, to be sure; nor should they be of too long continuance, if the end be to keep the *constitution* sound.

—— It may happen, indeed, Mr. Bull, that the people may be made to fast too often, whilst a flock of wolves are feasting upon their stock. The experiment is dangerous, and the minister who should make it, deserves the fate of *Behram's* vizier, not only as an enemy to the public, but also to his master, from whom he estranges the affections of his subjects. A king is neither more nor less than a chief magistrate, selected by and from the people, for the *public good;* and he who does not make that his chief business, is no king;—he who entrusts his people to a minister, without overlooking him, is a *mere bubble,* or, as a certain Spaniard had it, a *ceremony!*—This man had been sent out by Philip II. king of Spain, on an embassy; and the king finding fault with him for failing in an affair of great importance, because he could not agree with the French ambassador on some *etiquette,* said to him—*Como, a dexada una cosa di impor-tancia por una ceremonia! How, have you left a business of importance for a ceremony!* The ambassador boldly replied : *Como! por una ceremonia! Vuessa majesta misma no, es sin una ceremonia.—How! for a cere-mony!*[2] *your majesty's self is but a ceremony.* ——CHARLES XII. of *Sweden* (although himself a king, and not very well to pass for sense even among them) was so sensible of this, that when, after an absence of four-teen years from his capital, his regency, un-certain whether he was alive or not, wished to make peace with the czar of Russia, and king of Denmark, contrary to his inclina-tion, he wrote to them, that he would send them one of his *jackboots*, to which they might apply for orders!! Indeed where a king is such a madman as he showed himself to have been, happier would be the people if a *jackboot* filled up the *regal ceremony ;* espe-cially if the *king jackboot* should happen to have as faithful and able a minister assigned to it, as a certain *canine viceroy*, of which we are going to tell a story :

A KING OF TEN THOUSAND,

AND

A FAITHFUL MINISTER.

A CERTAIN Mandarin, who *Johor* rul'd,
  (Viceroy of SAON MAHON, Siam's king),
With such an iron rod the people school'd,
  That to the grind-stone they his nose did bring.

Proud, silly *Saon Mahon*, at the news,
  Splutters out two, or three great hearty d--mns :
" He'll make the *Johor women* bleat like ewes,
  " When cruel butchers take away their lambs."

Then off he march'd, with such prodigious force,
  As struck the men of *Johor* with dismay ;
They tamely saw each leader's mangled corse,
  Trampled by elephants, bestrew the way.

They also heard great *Saon Mahon* roar—
  " Vile reptiles ! since to anger thus ye dare
" Me, the *White Elephant's* dread king ; no more
  " A man shall rule ye, but my dog, I swear !

" Prostrate, ye wretches ! BARKOUT, thee we place
  " On Johor's throne—*our representative ;*
" With teeth and claws sway this rebellious race,
  " Who grumbles, not a moment let him live.

" MANI the post of *minister* shall fill,
  " Whose zeal by us so often has been tried."
Mani was wise ;—he knew the despot's will
  Was law ;—so, bowing humbly, thus replied:

" O mighty king of Siam, your viceroy
  " Will for his service find no want of zeal ;
" The master, he, his genius must employ—
  " The servants we, to guide the public weal."

Mani then turn'd towards the *dog*, and bow'd
  Thrice to the ground, and bark'd in humble tone ;
Barkout, with ears erect, replied so loud,
  No other *royal speech* so shook a throne.

The viceroy's eloquence, the premier's skill
  In languages, surpris'd the abject crew ;
With shouts of joy and loud acclaims they fill
  The air, and to the skies their turbans flew.

Nor vain their hopes ;—the docile dog was won
  By kindness to pursue sage Mani's plan ;
Ne'er slumber'd later than the rising sun—
  The *levée* o'er, the *council board* began.

Mani propos'd the question for debate,
  Each member freely his opinion spoke ;
The *viceroy* bark'd, and *Mani* did translate
  His wise decision—up the council broke.

Now to his *subjects*, patient audience giv'n,
   He prudent granted—courteously refus'd;
No minister and viceroy, under heav'n,
   So gen'ral satisfaction e'er diffus'd!

This done, they serv'd up dinner, neat but plain—
   A paunch, a pluck, sheep's-head, or some such things;
No ancient hero, Arthur, Charlemagne,
   Laid on so well—not even Homer's kings.

Next—out to exercise the troops he'd draw,
   Or, in the park, hunt to digest his meal;
Then sign dispatches with his well-ink'd paw—
   At once the *royal* signature and seal.

All business o'er—familiarly he barks
   With Mani, till the supper is prepar'd;
Then early goes to rest, to rise with larks,—
   Thus ev'ry day this *faithful guardian* far'd.

Such royal industry and temp'rance prov'd
   What good by good examples may be wrought;
Mani corrected, though he ne'er reprov'd,
   And into life the torpid province brought.

Good kings too soon are gone!—It so mischanc'd,
   A horde barbarian, from Malacca's coast,
Landing, spread death wherever they advanc'd—
   Barkout soon headed all his warlike host.

Knowing no more of tactics than a horse—
  Not more, perhaps, than our brave **** ** ****,
He left his generals'to take their course:
  'Twas wise—let soldiers do a soldier's work.

Not to be idle, through the ranks he ran,
  Arm'd only with brass collar, teeth, and claws;—
Charg'd, 'mongst the foremost, through the Malay van,
  And gave no quarter with his slaught'ring jaws. ·

The Malays fly—the Johor victor's shout—
  (Ah, cruel fate! why didst thou so ordain?)
A poison'd arrow strikes the brave *Barkout*—
  In vict'ry's arms he bites th' ensanguin'd plain.

The victors mourn'd their conquest too dear bought:
  Grief and despair throughout the province spread;
Sable-clad deputies the tidings brought
  To Siam's king, with *Mani* at their head.

Thus *Mani* spoke :—" Great king, that specter'd elf,
  " Grim death hath seiz'd our father, your viceroy;
" Nay, I had almost said, *your other self*—
  " Your gift inestimable, our sole joy!

" He for your people liv'd—in battle died;
  " In their defence, and for your glory slain;
" A *Mandarin successor*, swol'n with pride,
  " Would for good *Barkout's* loss renew their pain.

" *White Elephant's* dread king, then hear our pray'rs ;
  " Let no *man* rule us, as you did decree ;
" We'd have for viceroys only *Barkout's* heirs,
  " To his and thine we'd rather bend the knee."

Wise Saon Mahon scratch'd his head, full fraught,
  Whether 'twere best to follow up his whim :
If they're so fond of quadrupeds, he thought,
  They might prefer his *Elephant* to him.

This jealousy prevail'd—he feign'd good will,
  And said—" No more shall *Johor* feel disdain ;
" My place let *Mandarin Miracha* fill,
  " His former post good *Mani* shall retain."

Well, what turn'd up ? *Miracha* would not take
  Mani's advice ; and, striving to excel
Barkout, so widely did the way mistake,
  The *dog* he render'd more respectable.

The moral of this tale, according to the
Chinese account, in which the history of
Barkout is preserved, is this : " That next to a
prince who is willing and able to manage
himself the affairs of his government, the
most desirable is a monarch of indifferent
abilities, who will consent to be directed by
an able and well-intentioned minister."—We

readily acquiesce in this inference of the Chinese moralist; but we would wish to be informed how a king of indifferent abilities should know whether he has such a minister, unless he deign now and then to consult the people on that head. It would be absurd to ask the minister himself; because no man was ever known who entertained even an indifferent opinion of his own talents—witness our late *bread-bottomed* administration, whose blunders were palpable to the touch. We may also instance Mr. C—nn—g, among the present ministry, who asserts that the nation is at this moment rising, although he only imagines it to be the case, because (as S— F—— B—— told him) he was rising himself. Thus men intoxicated fancy that the room runs round, although it is only themselves that totter!—Hence is implied that a king and his people should talk *plain* language to each other, but in terms suited to their respective situations. This mode would naturally beget the greatest confidence and harmony, which could only be dissolved by what, in that case, there would be little reason to apprehend—foreign subjugation. When speeches and actions are designed to agree, it would be vain to attempt from abroad to embarrass our councils, and corruption, becoming useless, would consequently die away in our cabinet.

THE HEARTS OF THE PEOPLE ARE THE SECURITY OF EVERY ESTABLISHMENT!!

Those foolish kings, who assimilate themselves to the Creator, and despise their people, may be, and mostly have been, in turn, despised by them. For instance, on the garden front of the royal palace of Versailles, was formerly this inscription :

Hic fuit, ante, Chaos!
Dixit Ludovicus,
Et inde Regia fit Divo!
Facta est ita machina
Mundi.

Formerly,
Chaos reigned here!
Louis spoke,
And thence sprung a palace fit for a God!
So was formed the machine
Of the world!!!

The descendants of this heaven and world maker cannot, at present, boast a foot of this divine manufacture.

About the middle of the last century, an artist of Vienna constructed an automaton, dressed in the habit of an Austrian gentleman, with a pen in one hand, and a standish in the other; after dipping the former in the latter, it would strike a kind of spiral line upon a sheet of paper, and in the spaces between write these words: *Augustæ domini Austriacæ et Imperatori, Deus nec metas nec finem ponet.*—In English—*God will set neither bounds nor period to the House of Austria and the Emperor!* But Buonaparté, a petty Corsican adventurer, has already put bounds to the one, and will probably put a period to the other ere long, notwithstanding that his Imperial Majesty bought the wonderful piece of parasitical mechanism, and settled a considerable pension on the inventor. ——Who does not recollect, when the present emperor of Germany marched into Brussels, in the year 1794, to head the allied armies against the French, this remarkable inscription on the trophies:—" *Cæsar adest —trement Galli.*"—Cæsar is at hand—let the the Gauls tremble!——Who trembles now?

Surely there have been examples enough of this kind to have taught kings that they are but human beings, and, consequently, should bow with more reverence tó God, and behave with more becoming respect to their fellow-creatures. Crowns are not a more certain tenure than any other hereditary possessions, since both originate in, and owe their protection to, the laws of the land. They have been usurped; resumed by the people for implied breaches of contract and abdication; and they have been even *extended for the benefit of creditors,* of which the following notable precedent occurred in this metro-

polis:—THEODORE ANTHONY, Baron New-
hoff, and King of Corsica (who was as much
a king as any on the face of the earth, since
he was elected by the choice of the Corsi-
cans) was actually a prisoner in the Fleet,
and reduced to take the benefit of an act of
insolvency. Going to Guildhall to demand
the benefit of the act, he was asked, as usual,
what effects he had? and answered—" *Nothing but my kingdom of Corsica.*" It was
accordingly registered for the benefit of the
creditors!

It is lamentable to see the descendants of
kings who have been dethroned, and reduced
to the rank of subjects; but we are apt to
attach too much importance to such events:
The loss of an inheritance of five hundred
pounds a year only, is, *pari passu*, as
severely felt by the heir of a country squire,
as that of a crown can be by the heir of a
throne; because it is the *ne plus ultra* of both
their expectations, and perhaps of their ambition. In both instances, it is the instability
of human nature—the Divine decree—from

4

which even our Saviour was not exempted; and the only consolation is, that it is so, especially if the sufferer is not conscious of having deserved the chastisement. When the case is otherwise—where a king (to confine ourselves to our present subject) has broken his contract, or failed in his duty towards his people, there will be no resource for consolation within his own breast, nor will he experience any more pity from without, than the *drovers* of whom we are now about to give a story :—

THE OVER-DRIVEN OX.

It happens oft, on Smithfield market day,
    Some wanton drovers, for their cruel sport,.
Will goad an ox, which harmless holds its way,
    Till, stung with pain, it 'gins to foam and snort.

With joy the fiends behold the growing fun,
    And ply their sticks to keep the game alive;
" Mad Ox !" they shout; the beast sets out to run,
    And into shops or cellars people dive.

The brute, by worse brutes driven, raging falls
    On woman, man, or child, whate'er it meets,
O'erwhelms old women 'neath their apple-stalls,
    And with dismay and terror fills the streets.

An ox so goaded once, its error found
    To vent its rage thus on a flying crew ;
So on its fell pursuers turning round,
    High in the air the brace of drovers flew.

Then down they came, but not on *beds of down,*
    Nor *beds of roses,* but Scotch paving stones ;
None pitied them—a nuisance to the town—
    They very well deserv'd their broken bones.

2

MORAL.

Tis dangerous to urge, to any length,
A man, or beast, beyond their nat'ral strength;
Despair has often snapp'd the tyrant's chain,
And caus'd the slave his freedom to regain.

James II. of England, whose pretended legal massacres, by means of his bloody instrument Jefferies, justified what was said of him by Lord Churchill, that a marble chimney-piece was as capable of feeling compassion as the king's heart, afforded a remarkable instance of a haughty tyrant in prosperity, and of an abject coward in adversity. This unfeeling monarch received a most cutting stroke, at a council which was called soon after the landing of the prince of Orange, when, amidst the silent company, he applied himself to the earl of Bedford, father of the Lord Russel, whom he and his brother had brought to the block, saying— "My lord, you are a good man, and have great interest; you can do much for me at

this time."—To which the earl replied : " I
am an old man, and can do but little—(then
added, with a sigh)—I had once a son, who
could now have been very serviceable to your
majesty."——Which words, says Echard,
struck the king half dead with silence and
confusion.   Thus friendless, he was obliged
to take to his heels, and exist upon the scanty
bounty of the French king, and the kingdom
was happily delivered from the last of the
tyrannical and cruel, though weak dynasty
of the Stuarts.—Yes, *Jamie* ran

" *Over the hills and far awa'*—"

and was received by our *good friends*, the
French, in hopes of raising a civil war
amongst us ; and, as one good turn deserves
another, now, when they sent the Bourbon
dynasty to grass, we returned the compliment.   When examples, therefore, are as
plenteous as blackberries in autumn, why
will not kings take them, but on compulsion,
as children take physic, or horses drenches.
Why will they not remember that—

"———— Pigmies are pigmies still,
Though plac'd on Alps."—

Kings can only appear great through the
medium of their subjects' happiness ; without
their love, royalty is but an *ombre Chinoise;*
a single puff blows out the candles, and all
cats are grey in the dusk. To look down
from an elevated station is too apt to turn
weak heads giddy :—

"———— How fearful
And dizzy 'tis to cast one's eyes so low !
The crows and choughs, that wing the midway air,
Shew scarce so gross as beetles. Half way down
Hangs one that gathers samphire ; dreadful trade !
Methinks he seems no bigger than his head.
The fishermen, that walk upon the beach,
Appear like mice ; and yon tall anchoring bark
Diminish'd to her cock ; her cock a buoy
Almost too small for sight. The murm'ring surge,
That on th' unnumber'd idle pebbles chafes,
Cannot be heard so high."

SHAKESPEAR's LEAR.

Hence it is that a people, viewed at an immense distance below the throne, through the

misty medium of lying courtiers, are too often mistaken for the scum of a pot—a swinish multitude; and the " *murmuring surge,*" their remonstrances or petitions for redress of grievances " *cannot be heard so high.*" But there is a time for all things. James II. found not that pity to which he himself had ever turned a deaf ear; he despised his people without cause, and he was more than despised by them with the justest cause.

It is far easier to lose *rights* than to recover them, and therefore a *free* people ever are, and should be, extremely jealous of them. Such jealousy, far from giving pain to government, should afford it the utmost satisfaction and confidence, as men so tenacious of their own, will scarcely ever seize upon another's. They have no incitement to encroachment;—born to consider their own ease and happiness as the *summum bonum* of life, although they may be at times misled or abused, their judgments are always the sounder as they are devoid of a lust for power.

They more frequently lose ground, for want
of contending for it in time, than otherwise;
whilst *prerogative*, grasping what belongs to
it with one hand, and ever catching at more
with the other, goes on till it produces re-
monstrance, recrimination, and subversion.
Hence the source of all the revolutions that
are recorded in history! A people, driven
inch by inch to desperation, has no other
resource. It is not to be forgotten that had
the English nation been less tenacious of its
privileges, the House of Brunswick would
not have wielded the British sceptre, and it
concerns that House to be aware, that the
surest method to retain it is to cherish that
tenacity in the nation. When a government
complies with a reform of abuses with a good
grace, the people revere it, as if it had had
no hand in these abuses; nay, almost as if it
had bestowed new privileges upon them; but,
when it is extorted, they treat their conquered
oppressors as criminals. The heavy duties
incumbent on royalty are obvious; a king
must have assistance; and perhaps the most

arduous task of the whole is to choose a proper minister; above all, he should take care not to keep one who may, by his arrogance, alienate the affections of his subjects from him. Abuses in government occasion indigence in the governed; and the indigence of the people, says Mr. De St. Pierre, in his ' *Etudes de la Nature*,' is a mighty river, which is every year collecting an increase of strength, which is sweeping away before it every opposing mound, and which will issue in a total subversion of order and government. Royalty should set an example of magnanimity and disinterestedness, which should never suffer itself to be polluted by a *dealing in patronage*, which degrades it to the rank of a Moorfields broker. From royalty, as the source of *honors*, that is *titles*, every distinction should flow as freely as light from the sun. It may be doubted whether a king can receive the slightest present from a subject, or suffer any of his family to receive it, without lowering his dignity. Under a master resolved to maintain it, few ministers would dare to carry on a *traffic* in those *offices* which are to be filled solely for the benefit of the public, and the fees of which are solely paid by the public. They have a right to have them filled by men of ability and integrity, not speculators and brokers; they have a right to desire their removal, or even punishment, if they should prove incapable or knavish; but *purchase* renders them in a manner independent both of government and people. The former are necessitated to screen them, to keep their own *nefarious traffic* a secret from the latter. " *Minùs est quàm servis dominus, qui servos timet*"— says *Publius Syrus.—That master is less than a servant who fears his servants.* What can we think, then, of *royalty* committing itself before its *servants?* Besides the loss of respect, such degradation will give them encouragement to practise unbounded venality, and let loose every basest passion, to the corruption of the morals of the people, the evasion of all wholesome laws, the utter empoverishment of the middling and lower classes, and consequently the degeneracy and downfal of the whole nation.—The end of such a career must soon have been—" *Hic Tros fuit.*"—*Here Troy once stood.* Let us now hope that, as *Astræa,* the goddess of justice, has long since fled from earth to heaven, the *demon of corruption* has sculked to hell, whence it originally sprang.

THE DEVIL AND HIS IMP.

(Supposed to be taken from Canynge's Chest.)

THE *Demon* of *Corruption* fled
　To Hell, on sooty wings;
"Hey!" cries the *Devil,* "Whose *mare's dead?*
　" Why leave th' abode of *kings?*"

" I liv'd in glee," the demon cried,
　And then began to *wheeze*—
" Until by *Flintshire* hands I died,
　" Which choak'd me with *Welch cheese.*"

COURT BUBBLES.

"Well, of all plagues which make mankind their sport,
Guard me, ye heav'ns, from that worst plague, a court!
'Midst the mad mansions of Moorfields, I'd be
A straw crown'd monarch, in mock majesty;
Rather than sov'reign rule Britannia's fate,
Curs'd with the follies, and the farce of state.
Rather in Newgate walls, O let me dwell,
A doleful tenant of the darkling cell,
Than swell in palaces the mighty store
Of fortune's fools, and parasites of power;
Than crowns, ye gods! be any state my doom,
Or any dungeon—but a drawing-room!"

PAUL WHITEHEAD.

Ladies and gentlemen of the courtier tribe, ye are such wretched hacks, and such hacknied subjects, that it is scarcely possible to add a new epithet to that with which ye have been burthened for ages past. Ye are, indeed, too contemptible for notice, if ye were not the pests of courts, and the moths of society. Notwithstanding all the exploits of Alexander, who won several great victories, yet, in the latter part of his life, he became

considerably diminished from the magnanimous and modest youth which he came
out of the hands of Aristotle. He no sooner
threw himself open to the attacks of such
sycophants as you are, than he assumed
Divine honors, and disclaimed a really illus-
trious descent for a superstitious and fabulous
one, and committed those atrocities for which
he was put out of the world, as we now stifle
persons raging with the hydrophobia, for the
common safety.

Horace's praises of Augustus Cæsar are, at
the present day, read only for the beauty of
the poetry, as we glean from well-authenti-
cated historical facts, that he was every thing
but a great prince. At Actium, he hid himself in the hold of the ship, and did not
appear upon deck till the action was ended.
At Philippi, he left the camp, and feigned
illness, from a dream of his physician. His
cruelty, after the fight, to the prisoners, who
prayed only for a funeral, and his answer,
" that the birds of the air would soon put
them in a condition to have no need of any,"

prove him to have wanted that mercy towards a vanquished foe which distinguishes
the brave man from the cruel dastard. His
sacking of Perusia, which Lucius Antonius
took for him, and his massacre of three hundred senators there; his extreme avarice and
superstition—all prove him to have been a
weak man; yet at one of his luxurious feasts
in Rome, he caused nine women to be dressed
in imitation of the muses, and he himself ap-
peared in the character of Apollo. Some of
your *worthy* parasitical predecessors had
persuaded him that he was the son of that
god, and made out his pedigree thus:—that
he and Alexander were the sons of *two ser-
pents*, one of which was Apollo, and the
other Jupiter. If Alexander deserved to be
reckoned a madman, for wishing to pass for
a god, after so many great actions, in what
rank can we place this poltroon?—It is
almost to be lamented, that Horace's beau-
tiful but flattering portrait should have descended to mislead posterity. Like rats,
detested and pursued by almost every other

species, ye sculk securely through all the blind avenues of courts, and would grow fat but for your malignant envy towards each other.

Would to Heaven that every king had as prudent a treasurer, and as much Scotch economy as our James I.—That king, having ordered a present of twenty thousand pounds to one of his favorites, the treasurer, who was well read in human nature, and knew how little the general expression of things operated, and that the words *twenty thousand pounds* were as easily pronounced as *twenty thousand farthings*, contrived to place the whole sum in a heap before the king's eyes as he passed to the *levée* in new *Jacobuses.* When the king was taken from his generals to particulars, and saw the vast quantity of gold which he had ordered away for a trifle, he was frightened at what he was about, and, throwing one arm, in a vast agony, over the mass of gold, scrambled up with the other a *moderate handful*, and exclaimed, as if ashamed of his own folly—" *There, there,*

gi 'un that—that's enough."—Such *prudent housekeeping* would soon rid any palace of such useless and destructive vermin. If a lopping were now to be made of all useless places and pensions, and such as ought to remain were curtailed, according to James's Scotch economy—*" gi 'un that—that's enough"*—how many hundreds of those moles would be unsheltered, who at present riot on the public vitals, and are making such quick work with them—

> " As th' earth is easiest undermin'd
> By vermin impotent and blind."
>
> HUDIBRAS.

Enough of this *wholesale domestic warfare* (ten thousand times more to be deprecated than any foreign one, although against the world in arms) has already been brought to light, to sicken the imagination. Were the whole to be brought to light! That would be a tale indeed to *" harrow up the soul."*— Perhaps some honest man, as bold as his cause is just, may continue, or take up the task, already so well begun, of cleansing the Augæan Stable. Such a man as will disdain the stage-shifting, scene-changing, trap-door rising and sinking of a place-man, and patriot alternately, as occasion serves, or necessity compels, and will do his duty towards the public, in spite of the taunts or insinuations of such a serpent, although conscious that is too often the fate of a man

" ————— lab'ring to be good—
His honesty's for treason understood:
While some false flatt'ring minion of the court
Shall play the traitor and be honour'd for't."

If a man who strives to arrest the country on the brink of ruin is to be termed *Jacobin*, and those who lend a hand to drag the Cerberus sickening at the day, to public view, an *unprincipled association*, by a man without principle, or, to speak more properly, of the very worst principle that the finger of honesty can point at, it must be acknowledged to be a task Herculean, and that the public gratitude ought to equal the task. But of this hereafter. Let us make as quick work with the courtier tribe, as they are making with the constitution.

It is little consolation to a ruined nation that court sycophants cannot make kings ridiculous without making of themselves, at the same time, *things* such as God never created, nor intended to create—*things* at which the lowest degradation of mortality sneers. One of these things is very seldom seen out of its court burrow, lest, in its absence, some of its *friends* should cut its throat; but when it ventures abroad, its march resembles that of a crab, from its continued shuffling about, to avoid having its back towards royalty, which would be an unpardonable offence; and its sole business is to pick up falsehoods, scandals, or, at leisure, to invent them, to tickle the royal ear, or answer some private end. The most restive colt that ever was, never suffered half so much in the *manége*, as one of those *things* at its first court-breaking-in: Head, eyes, tongue, arms, legs, front, back, and sides, all move by clockwork;—but take a view of that ridiculous scene called a court ball.

At the upper end of the ball-room, under a canopy of state, sit the king and queen; and within a railing, erected for that purpose, forming a kind of oblong, stand all the nobility of a certain degree, as peers, peeresses, and their eldest sons and daughters. The secondary ranks, or the inferior nobility, placemen, their wives, and all such persons as, by their alliances or connexions, claim the title of *somebodies*, (that is the cant word for people of fashion, as that for the public is *nobodies*) are enclosed in like manner from the third rank, or royal tradesmen, with their wives, &c. *tout ensemble* not much unlike, in appearance, to a Smithfield *cattlepen*.

The ball opens with minuets, the parties, who have announced their wish to exhibit themselves, being called out according to the lord chamberlain's list. Then you behold every thing but Lord Chesterfield's *graces*. The narrow limits prescribed to the performers;—the vast extent of the ladies' hoops, (which make them resemble Astley's *pony-races*—or boys with their lower parts enclosed in wicker baskets, and covered with horse-cloths, to appear like ponies) together with the prohibition of turning their backs on royalty, which obliges them to spoil the figure, by dancing up into corners in front of majesty, instead of the proper graceful turning and crossings;—all these impediments create a scene laughable enough, although *etiquette* will not allow a laugh, nor even a grin, unless a smile appear on one of the royal faces, when it is expected to go round the company, like bumper toasts among convivials, although no one knows the cause of it.——After two hours passed in this tedious and *monotonous* (pardon the boldness of the figure) shuffling and grinning, the royal pair retire, and with them all restraint. The country dances then begin, and, at a certain time, the sideboard opens, when a general bustle and scramble ensue, to catch a morsel. To add to the confusion, the *perquisite*-mongers, dreading their courtier jaws, blow out the

4

candles with all expedition, to save as much as possible for themselves. Of late, however, the sideboard has never once made its appearance—to the great loss and grief of all parties concerned.——Such—such is the unvarying life of a courtier—for, *ex pede Herculem.* Chained to the royal whims, like galley-slaves to their oars, they tug and turmoil, hated by each other, execrated by the public, and despised by the royal personages, before whom they play the parts of *dancing-dogs,* as the following story will evince :—

THE KING,

COUNTRYWOMAN, AND COW.

A TRUE STORY.

HENRY the Fourth of France, marching in state,
    At head of all his fawning courtier crew,
(Just as a bell-wether, with curly pate,
    Conducts his tribe of lamb, and ram, and ewe)
        O'ertook a buxom country lass,
        And cow—she stopp'd to let them pass.

He lov'd with such like folks to have a word—
(No pride in him—no more than *George the Third*)
So ask'd what price she set upon her cow?
" *Six louis*, Sir—I can't take less, I vow."—
" Goody, too much"—" Lord, Sir, how can you tell?
" You're no *cow-dealer*—that I know full well."
" Goody, you're blind, or might have seen that plain,
" From this large *drove* of *calves*, I've in my train."

" Man may escape from rope and gun ;
  Nay some have outliv'd the doctor's pill;
Who takes a woman must be undone,
  That basilisk is sure to kill.

The fly that sips treacle, is lost in the sweets,
So he that tastes woman ruin meets."

MACHEATH—BEGGAR's OPERA.

When a prince ascends a throne with
wrong notions of the regal institution, ima-
gining the end of his station to be only his
own individual gratification, what conduct
is to be expected from him ? That which will
alienate the affections of his subjects, and,
consequently, expose his weakness to the
ridicule and contempt of his enemies. Those,
therefore, who are entrusted with the education of princes, are subjected to a responsibility of the first magnitude, since on them
may materially depend the happiness or
misery of a whole nation. We say *may*,
because though proper education will always
correct, it cannot always wholly counteract a
perverse nature: Witness Seneca's failure

with Nero. A prince, however, should be taught primarily, that God, who is Lord and King over all, proposes the happiness of all his people, and wills not that they should be oppressed; that to imitate God is the noblest part they can act; and that it is their indispensible duty to make mankind happy; since kings are placed over them solely that they may enjoy the fruits of their honest industry in peace and security. A prince, thus instructed, will make himself acquainted with the constitution of the country which he is to govern, and which, without this knowledge, it is impossible that he should govern as he ought to do. It is most remarkable that among nations, civilized or uncivilized, we know no instance where any individual is entrusted with the supreme power, until he has sworn to be faithful to his trust. A prince of Great Britain, previously to his being crowned, is obliged to " solemnly promise and swear to govern the people of the kingdom of England, and the dominions thereto belonging, according to the

statutes in parliament agreed on, and the
laws and customs of the same." Is it not
therefore incumbent, not only on the heir
apparent, but on all the princes of the blood
royal, who may, by any possibility, be
within the pale of the succession, to make
themselves acquainted with those statutes,
laws, and customs, according to which they
must promise and swear to govern? Certainly
—or we may again behold that paradox of
the governor governed, which has so often
proved fatal to weak kings, and their vile
ministers or favorites. Let us now merely
suppose an instance, that the next person in
succession to the throne, instead of qualifying
himself to perform his solemn promise and
oath, should have mispent his time with
idle and dissolute companions, in bagnios,
race-courses, gaming-houses, tennis-courts,
&c. &c., if his mind be not then relaxed,
and too much poisoned to apply itself to the
attainment of the knowledge of the arduous
and indispensible duties of the regal function,
still the executive has to go to school, and

the art of governing the most civilized and
most mercantile nation of the world, is not
so easy a task as to be conned over in two or
three years, during which time the bowl
must run according to the bias, be it delivered by a skilful or incapable hand.   Let
us now suppose, on the other hand, that, on
mounting the throne, the young monarch
should fancy himself trampling upon the
necks of a parcel of slaves, created only for
his own personal gratification and caprice, it
would be well for him if he should meet with
such a faithful and resolute adviser as another
young and mistaken king, of whom we are
about to relate an anecdote, before the current
of the popular indignation should have swept
him out into the ocean of contempt and oblivion.   While the shadow of freedom remained
in Portugal, the greatest men in that nation
were heroic and brave, and we find recorded
the following noble trait of this spirit :—

Alonzo IV. surnamed *The Brave*, ascended
the throne in the vigour of his age.   The
pleasures of the chace engrossed all his atten-

tion. His confidents and favorites allured
him to such pursuits, and encouraged him in
them. His whole time was spent in the
forests of Cintra, while the affairs of government were neglected, or executed by those
whose interest it was to keep their sovereign
in ignorance. His presence at last being
necessary at Lisbon, he entered the council-
chamber with all the impetuosity of a young
sportsman, and with great familiarity and
gaiety entertained his nobles with the history
of a whole month spent in hunting, fishing,
and shooting. When he had finished his
narrative, a nobleman of the first rank stood
up and thus addressed him : " Courts and
camps were allotted for kings, not woods a id
desarts. Even the affairs of private men
suffer when recreation is preferred to business; but when the whims of pleasure engross
the thoughts of a king, a whole nation is
consigned to ruin. We came hither for other
purposes than to hear the exploits of the
chace—exploits which are only intelligible
to grooms and falconers. If your majesty

will attend to the wants, and remóve the
grievances of your people, you will find
them obedient subjects: if not——" The
king, starting with rage and indignation,
demanded : " If not—what ?"—" If not,"
resumed the nobleman, in a firm tone, " *they
will look for another and a better king.*"

Alonzo, in the highest transport of passion,
expressed his resentment, and hastened out
of the assembly.   In a little while, however,
he returned calm and reconciled.   " I per-
ceive," said he, " the truth of what you say.
He, who will not execute the duties of a
king, cannot long have good subjects.   Remember that, from this day, you have
nothing more to do with Alonzo the sportsman, but with Alonzo the king."   His
majesty was as good as his promise, and
became, as a warrior and a politician, the
greatest of the Portugueze monarchs.   How
few sovereigns would have shewn so reasonable a pliability, and how few of them
have found such an adviser—rough indeed,
but seasonable and salutary !   Whoever ima-

4

gines that the throne was only intended for
the couch of repose and indolence, is a fool.
It is the seat of the first magistrate of a
people, who have entrusted their welfare to
his paternal auspices. Whoever would instil any other maxim into the mind of a
prince, is a viper to mankind, and a traitor.
to his prince and country. If there had
been fewer of these vipers, the world would
not have witnessed so many fatal examples of
the untimely, and violent deaths of kings. A
good king has no interest but what is in
common with his people; a bad king has
nothing in common with his people, nor
have they with him;—*the compact is dissolved!*

We will not stay here to prove that there
is a compact between king and people, (the
act of settlement is enough to prove that,
being an agreement between King William
and parliament, the same as between two
private individuals) but we say that it is the
duty of those, to whom the education of
princes is entrusted, to instruct them that it

is so. Mr. Locke treats it as a strange absurdity, that private gentlemen, of estates and fortune, should be ignorant of the *laws* of *tenures.* " It is their landed property, (says he) with its long and voluminous train of descents and conveyances, settlements, entails, and incumbrances, that forms the most intricate, and most extensive object of legal knowledge. The thorough comprehension of these, in all their minute distinctions, is, perhaps, too laborious a task for any but a lawyer by profession: yet still the understanding a few leading principles, relating to estates and conveyancing, may form some check and guard upon a gentleman's inferior agents, and preserve him, at least, from *very gross and notorious imposition.*"—Now, without meaning to convert a prince into a pettifogger, considering of how much greater importance is a crown than a manor, would it not be proper to make an insight into the *tenure* of a *throne,* some part of the education of a prince? It might prevent mistakes, and heart-burnings, between

king and people, as it would give the former
a true idea of his relative situation with the
latter, an idea, which few kings have enjoyed
the happiness of having had properly in-
stilled into them. If it would prove of no
other service, it would, at least, tend to keep
princes out of those *disgraceful* amusements
which make them the associates and equals of
blacklegs, and the '*which way did the bull
run?* of every *Pat-hod-carrier!*'—Take an
example:—A letter from Paris says, " our
amusement of horse-racing continues still;
there were two the day before yesterday.
The first between the *Prince de Nassau*, and
the *Marquis de Fenelon*; who both *rode
their own horses.* The race was for four
hundred louis d'ors; but the imprudence of a
spectator was the cause of the marquis losing
his wager, and very near his life with it.—
His horse fell, and the marquis, who was
under him, received a violent hurt on his
head. The other race was between the *Duke
of Chartres*, and the *Duke of Lauzun.*
The Duke of Chartres's horse, which won

two former races, was beat this time by that of the Duke of Lauzun; their *grooms* rode this race, which was for two hundred louis d'ors."—So that the *princes* were the first spectacles of the gaping throng, and the grooms the second; which *distinction* does not subtract much from their *equality*.

The French nation, frivolous as it was, saw with indignation the behaviour of these *princes* of the blood, who not only rode their own horses, but entered into all the low dissipations of the turf. They exercised their whips on the spectators, as well as on their horses; and not only encouraged the officers to maltreat the crowd, but employed such grossness of speech, and horrid oaths, as shewed them not to be unskilled in the *slang* or vulgar tongue of the lowest blackguards in the nation. Not satisfied with exhibiting themselves as jockies, they exposed themselves to the ridicule of Paris by a *foot-race*. The Duke de Chartres, the Duke de Lauzun, and the Marquis of Fitzjames, betted five hundred louis which could first reach Ver-

sailles on foot. Lauzun *gave in* about half
way; Chartres about two thirds; Fitzjames
arrived in an exhausted state, and was hailed
conqueror by the Count d'Artois. He,
however, like a hero, nearly expiring in the
arms of victory, was put to bed and bled,
and gained his wager and an asthma. The
late queen of France carried her *refinement*
still farther, and instituted *ass-races*, be-
stowing on the winner three hundred livres
and a *golden thistle*, not with a view, we suppose, to burlesque our order of that denomi-
nation, but merely allusive to the plant to
which asses are partial.

How soon these *princes* came to the *end*
of their *race-course* is too well known!—At
this distance of time, we are induced, by the
irresistible pleasantry with which Shakespear has given of the excesses of *Prince
Henry*, (afterwards King Henry V.) to laugh
against our sober reason ; and the subject is
greedily laid hold of by those *vipers*, (whom
we have before designated as the *courtier-
bubbles*) to draw a *prince* into, and gloss over

those vices to which they themselves are most prone; and to debase him, until they have gained an entire ascendancy over him. " Henry," say they, " was a wild prince, but a great king." With all deference to truth, we think that he was as bad a king as he was a prince. In the first year of his reign, he was weakly led by the nose by the clergy ; (who, whether Pagan, Mahometan, or Christian, have been ever lusting after power, and the greatest enemies to the national liberties of the people,) to connive at the murder of the righteous and learned Old-castle, Lord Cobham, and hundreds of others, upon silly distinctions in points of faith, (which are now the ridicule of every body— even bigots) as they pretended, but in reality, because he had procured two bills to be brought into parliament against their *continual wasting of the temporalities*. Finding the king a *fit tool*, and a third bill to the like purpose being on foot in the parliament at *Leicester*, in order to distract the attention of the king and people from their own *prodi-*

gious extortions, oppressions, and *embezzle-
ments,* " they put the king in remembraunce
to claime his *right in Fraunce,* and graunted
him thereunto a disme, with other great sub-
sidy of money. Thus," saith the report
of his trial, (vide State Trials,) " were Christes
people betrayed, and their lives bought and
sold by these most cruell thieves. For in
the said parliament, the king made this most
blasphemouse and cruell acte, to be as a law
forever, That whatsoever they were that should
rede the Scriptures in the *Mother Tong,*
(which was then called *Wickleve's* learning)
they shud forfet land, catel, body, lif, and
godes, from they, their heyres forever, and so
be condempned for heretykes to God, enne-
mies to the crowne, and most errant trayters
to the lande."—The consequence of this
weakness of the king, was not only the massacre of hundreds of his best subjects, at
home, in cold blood, but his leading some
thousands to France to be knocked on the
head, or perish through disease, and the
utter empoverishment of the nation. All

these *worthy deeds* he contrived to effect within the short reign of nine years, and this is the *great example* which is held up to princes, who are to be seduced, and infatuated by those mercenary parasites—those

> " False flatt'rers that with royal goodness sport,
> Those stinking weeds that over-run a court."
>
> OTWAY.

whom may God for ever confound!

The following characteristic will serve as a mark on these *animals* to all those princes who may read our work, which, for their benefit more than our own, we hope many will do. As *Prince Maurice* was one day at dinner, a *dog* came in, and took sanctuary under the table. The pages beat him out of the room, and kicked him; but, for all that, *Monsieur Chien* came punctually at the same hour next day, and so continued his visits, though they continued the same treatment to him. At last the prince ordered them to beat him no more, adding, with a smile, that he was now convinced two of a trade could never agree, and the dog knew his trade better than any of them. From that time the dog commenced *perfect courtier*, followed the prince wherever he went, lay all night at his chamber-door, ran by his coach-side as duly as one of his lacquies; in short, so insinuated himself into his master's favour, that, when he died, he settled a pension on him for life!—The resemblance, however, goes no farther than the *assiduity* and *fawning*; in point of *fidelity*, the dog has the best of it out and out.

If princes suffer themselves to be led away by such fawning spaniels into deeds unworthy of them; into an association with blacklegs, on the turf, at the hazard or billiard tables, or in the tennis-courts; or are seen in public, arm in arm with police officers, and hand in glove with sheriff's officers, such conduct must *wither* their dignity, and leave only the blighted barren trunk, naked and disgusting to the eye. It is not altogether to be supposed that princes should be confined within the narrow circle of morality of men of inferior rank and fortune; but still they should remember, that the gratifications of private persons are out of their private purses ; theirs from the public purse, which has already too many hands in it;—that there are modes of conduct, which will render them inferior to the meanest of mankind. If, to gratify vicious passions in excess, recourse must be had to making a sale of royal favours, conferring honorable distinctions on dishonorable men, and lucrative places on usurers, bailiffs, necessitous prostitutes, and their more infamous paramours and pensioners, *the post of honor will,* indeed, *be a private station !!*

Affability and condescension are laudable qualities in princes; but it should never descend to familiarity, as it is one of the drawbacks on royal blood, that it cannot entertain friendship, which can exist only where there is equality. A prince's affability should seem to remove the barrier between him and the person with whom he converses, but should ever be ready to let it become apparent on the slightest approach to familiarity. A prince should be a *patron of men of modest merit*, and not a *pigeon* for *gamesters* to deplume.

It has been thrown out as a reproach on Mrs. Clarke that, to get rid of a just debt due to Mr. Few, she pleaded *coverture*; but, with all due deference, it is as much more disgraceful to a prince, as there is difference between his rank and hers, to plead the *sanctuary of a palace*, to defeat a just creditor! Every one must remember Æsop's fable of the poor cully with his two loving wives, one of whom plucked the white hairs out of his head, and the other the black, until, at last, they made him bald. *Falstaff* observes to *Prince Henry*, when playing the part of his father, and chiding him in *burlesque*: —"There is a thing, Harry, which thou hast often heard of, and it is known to many in our land by the name of *pitch ;* this pitch, as ancient writers do report, doth defile ; so doth the company thou keepest."

If princes associate with the vilest part of
mankind, they are themselves the *real jaco-
bins*, the *levellers* of *all distinctions*. The
attachment of every state to its government
must be in proportion to the protection
which it receives from it, in its property,
which word combines its ease, enjoyment,
and happiness. We can have no idea of
attachment to a tyrant, or to a profligate
prince, who evinces no feelings for his subjects. Families decay—communities never
die. " Nature," as Buffon observes, " is not
concerned about the preservation of the indi-
.viduals of any species ; but peculiarly interests herself in the preservation of the species
itself. The welfare of a community, which
combines thousands of families, must, in
like manner, be more important than that of
any individual family in it, being all equally
the creatures of, and of equal consequence to,
the Creator." For this reason, it is invariably
recorded in history, that a series of weak
princes never fail to work the dissolution of

their dynasty. They fall unprotected by God—unpitied by man. What has been the *attachment* of the continental European nations to their royal houses? What attachment could they have to them? They have repaid apathy with apathy, which can be a matter of astonishment to none but shallow reasoners. They have had *separate interests,* or rather they have had no interest, and, consequently, nothing to contend for. Fighting is not so pleasant an exercise that *men* should go to it for nothing, or what is worse, for those who oppress them. The continental princes have done Buonaparté's business for him, and their own too pretty well. I much question whether an English country 'squire would exchange conditions with either of them. Posterity will scarcely credit the historical reports of the present times, when it will seem as if it rained crowns only on the heads of fools, to show men of sense how little is their intrinsic worth. When Buonaparté tells the Spanish nation, that *he has diminished the number of monks—that he has*

abolished the Inquisition, which was a sub-
ject of complaint to Europe and the present
age—that he has abolished those privileges
which the grandees usurped—feudal rights,
and that henceforth every man may set
up inns, ovens, mills, employ himself in
fishing and rabbit-hunting, and give free
scope to his industry, he talks as a prince
ought to talk to his subjects, be his motive
what it may. It signifies very little to a
man from what source good flows, so it
does but come into his channel. A refor-
mation would be not a whit the less accept-
able for coming through Mrs. Clarke, or
any such impure medium. We would as
soon be beholden to her, as any other person, for reforming clerical abuses; revising,
tempering, pruning the too exuberant penal
statutes; curtailing immense farms, whereby
a home and bread would be given to thousands, and abolishing our game-laws, those
disgraceful remains of a tyrannical and obso-
lete system, as unjust as impolitic, in a
nation, which, from its contiguity to a most

potent rival nation, must ever have arms in
its hand. We repeat that we would rejoice
to be beholden to Mrs. Clarke, or any other
person whomsoever, and, as the lawyers
phrase it, of what nature or description whatsoever, for these and numerous other blessings
which could be pointed out, and are much
wanted. England should not be now, as—

> " ——————— In ages past,
> A dreary desart, and a gloomy waste,
> To savage beasts, and savage laws a prey,
> And kings more furious and severe than they."
>
> POPE.

In spite of the present gloomy aspect of
affairs, it must be evident to any one who will
look into futurity, that Europe will be considerably advantaged by getting rid of some
of its *old customs,* alias *prejudices,* or, in
more appropriate terms, *marks of the chain
of the dark ages;* and Britons, whose courage
and constancy have proved its bulwark against
Gothic tyranny, should not be the last to par-
take of the reward of their arduous labours.
Individuals ought to be protected by every

4

good government in the fruits of their industry, from which the laws of every well regulated police can expect them to contribute no more than what is necessary to the benefit of the community, and not to the maintenance of Jew lords, Jew members, Jew contractors, blacklegs, pimps, and prostitutes; in short, of all those in the lump, who fatten on the public purse, without being of the least reciprocal service to the country. ——Wipe me these off with a wet sponge, and we shall be once more much better acquainted with what the French term, the *poule au pot*, and more strangers to tax-gatherers, for which thousands of honest Britons daily pray, and, Heaven knows, with occasion enough.—The privations of the people, their reverence for religion, their love of the constitution, and their loyalty, are as notorious for their real existence, as the cries of No Popery—No Jacobinism—are for their being chimeras and phantoms raised by, intriguers, who, like *divers* in the streets, never fail of some humbug story, or device,

to create a throng, and then fall to picking
of pockets. In short, from what has al:
ready transpired on *investigation*, it would
be appropriate enough to place over the
door of a certain house in Downing-street,
a board, on which should be inscribed the
words: *Steel traps and spring guns set here
for the benefit of British legs and members.*
—What more may transpire we can pretty
well know, but hope that the necessity and
nauseousness of any farther *investigation* may
be spared to the country by the present in-
terval of cool consideration, and a proper
attention to the feelings of the country, whose
generosity, in that case, would be happy to
consign the past to the gulf of oblivion, in
which their own interest has so long lain
floundering.—We have had enough of *investigation*: " PRAY YOU AVOID IT."

THE PLAGUE AMONG THE BEASTS.

A FABLE.

THE Beasts, by dreadful plague once scourg'd,
To seek some remedy were urg'd;
The *Lion*, in this consternation,
Issues a *Royal Proclamation*,
Sending unto *His People Greeting*,
And calling for a solemn meeting.
When they were gather'd round his den,
He spake: " *My Lords and Gentlemen*,
" No doubt this deep affliction's sent
" On us, for our sin's punishment.
" To know why we are thus distrest
" Let each one straightway search his breast,
" And honestly confess his crimes,
" That to obtain more healthy times,
" In sacrifice the worst beast giv'n,
" May stop the vengeance just of Heav'n:
" And, as not one is free from sin,
" My own confession I'll begin:
" Through hunger, bulls and cows I've slain;
" With horses, goats, I've strewn the plain;
" Devour'd whole flocks of lamb and mutton,
" And e'en on shepherds play'd the glutton——"

Then stopp'd—"What harm," cries Chancellor Fox,
" Is there in that? What is an ox,
" A horse, sheep, goat, or such like things,
" But, *jure divino*, sport for kings?
" They're good for nothing but to eat,
" And royal jaws must not want meat ;
" And, being all your vassals born,.
" At your high will are to be torn,
" The shepherd, being your enemy,
" To kill him Nature sets you free.
" This, if our vote you'll put us on,
" *Your Parliament* will vote *nem. con.*"

In turn, the circling throng confess
All had been rogues, or more, or less;
But to each other complaisant,
And *liberality* their cant,
The great rogues wip'd off all abuses,
By the most frivolous excuses.
The tiger, leopard, wolf, and bear,
Whitewash'd each other, clean and fair
As Y——'s D——e, P——l, or W——y,
G——e R——e, H——n, C——gh;
And though their shame they could not smother,
Each call'd the other—*honest brother*.

At last, an *Ass*, a silly wight,
Confess'd that, almost starv'd, one night

VOL. I.   K

Chancing a church-yard wall to pass,
He pluck'd a little sour grass.
" Oh !" cried *Judge Wolf*," these are the crimes
" Have brought on us these dreadful times ;
" This profane, sacrilegious ass,
" Must die for munching *holy grass*."
All join'd the outcry, glad to pack
The saddle on another's back.

MORAL.

What signifies *investigation*—
Great rogues can blind, or awe a nation.

END OF VOL. I.

Printed by J. D. Dewick,
46, Barbican, London.

Lightning Source UK Ltd.
Milton Keynes UK
UKHW021912290421
382872UK00003B/118